Brides

By

Graysen Morgen

2014

Brides © 2014 Graysen Morgen

Triplicity Publishing, LLC

ISBN-13: 978-0990813316
ISBN-10: 0990813312

All rights reserved. No part of this publication may be reproduced, distributed, or transmitted in any form without permission.

This is a work of fiction. Names, characters, places, and incidents are the product of the author's imagination and are used fictitiously. Any resemblance to actual persons, living or dead, business establishments, events of any kind, or locales is entirely coincidental.

Printed in the United States of America

First Edition – 2014

Cover Design: Triplicity Publishing, LLC

Interior Design: Triplicity Publishing, LLC

Also by Graysen Morgen

Bridesmaid of Honor (Brides Series book 1)

Crashing Waves

Cypress Lake

Falling Snow

Fast Pitch

Fate vs. Destiny

In Love, at War

Just Me

Love, Loss, Revenge

Natural Instinct

Secluded Heart

Submerged

Acknowledgements:

Special thanks to my eagle eyes down under for swooping in and helping me whip this story into shape!

Thank you to Morgan, who also worked hard pointing out all of the common mistakes that I repeatedly made.
Multas gratias!

Dedication:

This book is dedicated to my mate, CJ. You've done so much to help me improve my writing in the past two years and you've become a great friend as well.
Si la vida es un libro de capítulos, y luego grandes capítulos deben seguir los malos, así que aquí tiene a otro gran capítulo de tu libro.

As always, to my partner, my best friend:
Te quiero más cada día.

Brides

Chapter 1

The gunmetal gray Porsche sped into the parking lot, nearly skidding to a stop between the freshly painted, bright white lines of a parking space. The driver's door swung open and Britton Prescott climbed out, dressed impeccably in a tailored black pantsuit and a crème colored button down blouse. The cool breeze blew her wavy chestnut hair around as she shut the door. She ran her hand through it and swept it over her shoulder in one quick, sexy swoop as she walked towards the small crowd gathered nearby.

"Can you get anywhere on time?" Bridget whispered harshly.

"I'm fashionably late," Britton teased her sister as she walked by.

"Hey, babe," Daphne smiled at her girlfriend.

Britton stepped closer, placing her hand on Daphne's waist. She leaned in for a quick kiss before walking towards the head of the group.

Everyone was gathered outside of the Prescott's Grocery headquarters for the unveiling of the new building. The construction had taken a little over six months to complete and Britton was glad to be putting this project behind her, but she still hadn't been given a full-time position with the design firm she was working for and she was starting to get more and more nervous as the days went by.

"I'm glad you decided to join us," her mother said with a raised eyebrow.

"I was tied up on a new project and lost track of time," Britton answered.

"Can I have your attention, please? Now that everyone is here," Stephen Prescott looked over at his youngest daughter. "I'd like to thank you all for coming out today to help us open the doors to the new Prescott's headquarters. Nine months ago, when I told my daughter, Britton, that I was thinking of building a new office building and wanted her to put some sketches together for me, I never thought I'd actually go through with the build. Now, here I am about to open the doors after less than a year. This building is everything Prescott's stands for: professional, efficient, and family oriented. As you all know, Prescott's has been in business over a hundred years and we plan to be open a hundred more. I want to say thank you to my family and the wonderful people at Walcott Construction for enduring these last six months with me. I know it hasn't been easy. I also want to extend my deepest gratitude to my daughter, Britton Prescott. Britton, you've proved this old man wrong in so many ways. I'm very proud of you." He smiled and held his hand out to her.

Britton stepped up next to him and helped him cut the yellow ribbon blocking the doors.

"Ladies and gentlemen, I give you Prescott's headquarters," Stephen said, stepped back with his arms spread. "Go on in. Champagne is being served here in the lobby. You're welcome to have a look around at all of the floors."

Brides

"Thank you, Daddy." Britton smiled and hugged him.

"I meant what I said. You're very good at what you do."

"Thanks." Britton was happy to see some of the light returning to her father's eyes. She knew she could never replace the disappointment he'd had from her not wanting to run the family business and she'd literally broken his heart when she'd given up everything, including a possible Olympic team spot, to go to design school, but having him finally acknowledge her career and talent was a huge start.

Britton grabbed a glass of champagne. She'd didn't need to explore the building, she'd been all around the inside of it so many times, she could lead a tour blindfolded. So, she mingled with a couple of the company employees she knew until she spotted Bridget and Daphne in the corner, talking to people she didn't recognize.

"Now that this huge weight is off your back, don't you think it's time you took the next step?" Sharon Prescott said.

Britton turned to face her mother. "And what exactly is the next step? The firm still hasn't hired me on full time. They haven't given me any indication that they are planning to either."

Sharon shook her head. "I'm not talking about the firm."

Britton looked at her mom with a puzzled expression. When her mother nodded in Daphne's direction, Britton blew out a frustrating breath.

"Mom, we haven't even been dating a year. Marriage is the last thing on my mind."

"It should be the first. That girl loves you and you love her. You've known her most of your life. What the hell are you waiting for? Her to ask you?"

Britton brushed her hair off her shoulder and grinned at Daphne when she saw her looking back at her. She did love her, more than anything in the world, but marriage was a huge step, one she'd never wanted to take with anyone.

"I don't know. I may be unemployed any day now, since this project is completed. I just don't think it's the right time. Besides, I don't even know if she wants to get married. We haven't really talked about anything like that and I'm not a fan of marriage."

"Britton Marie, I told you once already, if you let her get away—"

"Mom—" Britton started, but was cut off when her cell phone rang. She excused herself and stepped outside. The last thing she wanted to do was have another conversation with her mother threatening to cut off Britton's inheritance if she screwed things up with Daphne.

"Hey, how did the unveiling go?" Heather asked when Britton answered.

"Fine," Britton sighed.

"You don't sound too enthused."

"I was about to chew my mother out when you called."

"That's not good. Can you get away for lunch?" Heather asked.

Britton checked her watch. "Probably. Everyone else is having rubber chicken for lunch here. I'll tell them I'm needed back at the office. I'll see you at Booker's Deli in half an hour," she said, hanging up the phone.

Brides

"Is everything okay?" Daphne asked when she saw Britton walk back inside.

"Yeah. I need to get out of here. My mother's making me crazy. I'm going to go have lunch with Heather, but as far as you know, I'm needed back at the office to meet a client."

"I don't like lying," Daphne scolded.

"You had no problem with it when you were hiding that big rat in your closet!" Britton winked.

"Britton!" Daphne gasped.

"Walk me out," Britton nodded towards the door.

Daphne waited as Britton said her pleasant goodbyes, then walked out to the parking lot with her. Britton wrapped her arms around Daphne's waist and leaned back against the door of her sports car.

"I love you, you know that, right?" Britton sighed, placing her chin on Daphne's shoulder.

"Yes. What's gotten into you?" Daphne asked, running her hands through Britton's hair and resting them on her shoulders.

"I don't know. I'm stressed out I guess." Britton kissed her neck softly, working her way back to her lips for a passionate kiss that made them both weak in the knees.

Daphne slid her hands from Britton's shoulders to her chest above her breasts, pushing against her slightly.

"We can't do this here. Everyone's probably watching through the windows," Daphne chided, stealing one last quick kiss before backing away far enough to put some space between them.

Britton shrugged. "It'll give them something to masturbate to later," she laughed.

"Oh, gross!" Daphne shook her head, grimacing. She turned to walk away and looked back at Britton, smiling brightly.

Britton's body missed the warm, full-on contact of having Daphne against her and she knew she had better go before she pulled her close again.

~

Heather was sitting at their usual table, perusing the menu she knew by heart, when Britton slid into the opposite side of the booth.

"What's going on? Is there a problem with the building?" Heather asked.

Britton ordered a glass of wine. She'd only had half a glass of champagne at the unveiling, but as far as the firm knew, she was spending the rest of the day with her family at the party for their new office building.

"No, the building's fine. It's my mother I want to strangle."

"You're starting to sound like me with the stepmonster. You're mother's a sweetheart, albeit a little too prim and proper for her own good most of the time. What's she done to make you so upset?"

"She's pressuring me to marry Daphne."

"That's no big surprise."

"She's threatening me with my inheritance and she knows I could lose my damn job at anytime. Those fuckers still haven't come to the table with an offer. She thinks this will make me run to the next ring shop I drive past," Britton huffed.

"Oh," Heather sipped her raspberry tea.

"Oh?" Britton raised her eyebrows.

Brides

"What?"

"That's all you have to say?"

"Well, I want you guys to get married too. You're great together. I also know you hate the idea of marriage and have done your best to steer clear of any relationship that would lead to it."

"Seriously? You think I'm not committed?"

"I didn't say that, Britt, but think about it. You strung that, whatever you call it with Victoria, on long enough to get past a couple of years without ever thinking about marriage. Now, you're in a serious relationship and you're obviously head over heels in love with each other. Marriage kind of is the next step."

"We haven't even been dating a year and we don't even live in the same state! Why does everyone think we have to get married right this damn minute?" she growled.

A few people at nearby tables turned their heads in Britton's direction.

"Calm down. I didn't say you need to run to the altar before the end of the month, but you should start thinking about the future."

"Future? If it were up to my mother, we would've been married months ago. I wish everyone would just leave me alone about it. Daphne and I haven't even talked about marriage, or even moving in together for that matter." Britton drank half of the wine in her glass in one long sip.

"How about a change of subject?" Heather asked, seeing the frustration on her best friend's face.

"I'd love one."

Heather laughed. "How's the house coming?"

"I'm still on the very first rough draft. The idea has been in my head for as long as I can remember, but I'm having difficulty putting it on paper. It's not like I can build it anytime soon; at least, not until my career is stable anyway."

"What does Daphne think about it?"

"It was her idea. She asked me recently, if I could build anything I wanted without anyone's rules or concepts getting in the way, what would I build. So, I told her about my dream house. I also told her that's why I choose to live in an apartment because the only house I ever want to live in is one I design and build."

"Do you see her living there too?"

Britton raised an eyebrow at her best friend. "I'm not the asshole you're making me sound like. Of course I see her in my life. Does that mean we need to run to the altar? We're happy. Everyone knows we love each other. Why do we have to have a damn piece of paper to prove it?" Britton grimaced. "See, you have me talking about marriage again."

Heather shrugged. The rest of their lunch went by peacefully with a conversation about Heather's husband, Greg and his poker buddies. Britton didn't have a buzz since she'd only had the single glass of wine, yet she still didn't feel like going back to her office. Instead, she drove over to the arts and crafts store to grab some more drawing supplies and headed home.

Chapter 2

It was after five when Daphne used her key to get into Britton's apartment. She'd been surprised to see her car in the parking lot when she drove in, expecting her to still be at the office. Britton had charcoal and pencil sketches sprawled out over the kitchen table and she was dressed comfortably in an old t-shirt and a pair of short shorts.

"Hey," Britton said, looking up from the drawing in front of her and smiling with adoration for the woman standing a few feet away.

Daphne bit her bottom lip as she moved closer. Britton slid her chair back far enough for Daphne to straddle her legs.

"Why do I find this nerdy side of you so damn hot?" Daphne gasped between passionate kisses as she pulled Britton's t-shirt over her head and tossed it to the floor.

"I don't know, but I like it," Britton replied, unbuttoning her blouse and pushing it off her shoulders and down her arms.

Daphne bit Britton's lower lip playfully as she pushed her hand down between them, slipping it under the waistband of her shorts. Britton tossed Daphne's satin bra to the floor as she spread her own legs to allow Daphne's fingers to continue exploring. She tried to loosen Daphne's dress slacks enough to get her hand inside, but they were bunched up too tight because of their position.

"Uh-uh," Daphne said, shaking her head no and claiming Britton's lips for another powerful kiss. "I started this and I plan to finish it," she murmured breathlessly as she slid her fingers over Britton's clit, feeling the warm wetness she knew was waiting for her.

Britton flung her head back, groaning at the pleasure she was receiving as Daphne moved her fingers in a slow, steady rhythm. Daphne ran her tongue over Britton's lower lip, moving to place delicate kisses over her neck and shoulder, before going back to her ear.

"I've wanted to touch you all day," Daphne whispered. "When you were cutting the ribbon, I pictured you naked against those glass doors as I slid my fingers in and out of you with everyone watching."

"Oh God," Britton panted as her body writhed under Daphne's weight in her lap.

Daphne kissed her hard, grinning seductively when she saw the lust in Britton's gray eyes. Britton caught her breath and stood up with Daphne's legs wrapped around her. She laid her back on the table on top of her drawings and snatched her pants down, tossing them to the floor. She wasted no time, spreading Daphne's legs and going right for the glistening wet folds awaiting her tongue.

Daphne grabbed Britton's hair, tugging softly as Britton teased her with her tongue in long languid strokes.

"Please, baby," she panted, raising her hips and urging her further.

Britton wrapped her arms around Daphne's legs, fanning her hands over her abdomen as she sucked and

Brides

licked harder, sliding her tongue in and out of her with each pass. Britton's gray eyes locked onto Daphne's green ones as Daphne trembled against her.

Daphne put both hands on Britton's head, holding her mouth where she wanted it as she rode the wave of orgasm crashing over her. Unwilling to relinquish her body, she held on as the second orgasm hit her hard, causing her to roar like a caged animal.

Britton pulled her mouth away and grabbed a hold of Daphne's waist, pulling her back down into her lap on the chair behind her. Daphne's wet crotch soaked her shorts as their lips met in a passionate kiss. Britton wrapped her arms tightly around Daphne and Daphne threaded her fingers through Britton's long, wavy hair, resting them at the base of her neck.

"I love you so damn much," Daphne whispered.

"I love you too." Britton smiled. She waited a few minutes, taking the time to simply hold the woman in her arms. "So, naked against the office building, huh?" she teased.

Daphne's face blushed with embarrassment.

Britton shook her head. "If those people only knew the real you."

"What's that supposed to mean?" Daphne shrieked.

Britton shrugged. "You're like the shy, innocent young school teacher who's really a boudoir dominatrix who likes an audience."

"Oh, I am not!" Daphne smacked her shoulder playfully. "I'm about as far from both of those as you could get." She shook her head. "Dominatrix, really?" she laughed, still shaking her head.

Britton laughed. "Well, since you marked your territory on the new house, do you want me to add in a boudoir room for you?"

"What's that supposed to mean?"

Britton looked around her towards the table.

"Are those the sketches of your house?"

"Yes, and it looks like it will be *our* house."

Daphne noticed they were in disarray and two of them had large wet spots. She grinned sheepishly.

"It's been pussy-marked. No other woman is going to want to live there with me," Britton said seriously.

"Oh my God," Daphne laughed. "You're a mess." She started to get up, but Britton held her down. "Aren't you hungry?"

"I just ate." Britton grinned.

Daphne rolled her eyes. "Well, I didn't and Ying's sounds really—"

"Ying's can wait," Britton said, standing up with Daphne's naked body wrapped her around her when her cell phone rang loudly. Ignoring it, she continued down the hall towards her bedroom.

Chapter 3

Britton didn't check her voicemail until early the next morning when she was on her way to the office. Her father lad left a message asking her to come to Sunday brunch. She wasn't sure what it was for. Her parents didn't have casual get-togethers. Britton hit the Bluetooth button on her steering wheel as she downshifted for a red light.

"Good morning, sunshine," Heather yawned into the phone.

"I've been summoned to the family home for Sunday brunch."

"Uh-oh. What did you do now?"

"Nothing...at least nothing that I know of. If this is another ploy from my father to try and get me to come to work for him, I'm going to lose it."

"Is that what you think it is?" Heather asked.

"I have no idea. Why? Do you think it's something else?" Britton questioned.

"I don't know. They're your parents. Mine simply pick up the phone and say hey, blah-blah-blah and hang up. Yours sends out a damn formal invitation and expects your horse and buggy to arrive promptly with twenty minutes to spare."

Britton laughed so hard she nearly ran off the road.

"In all seriousness, do you think maybe it's about Daphne?"

"What about her? My parents think she's great and my mom is practically calling Daphne her daughter-in-law already. If it wasn't for the sex, I'd think my parents loved her more than I did. Especially, my mother."

"That's my point. Do you think they're going to push you to get married? Didn't you say something about your inheritance?"

"If that's what this is about, they can shove that inheritance up their asses. I'll get married if and when I'm God damn good and ready. They didn't push Bridget to get married to Wade. They dated for almost two years before he even proposed to her."

"I don't know, babe. I wish I had a better answer for you."

"I know," Britton sighed.

"Does Daphne know about this?"

"No. They're my parents. I'll deal with them. She's still having issues with her own accepting our relationship."

"Yeah, mom told me she had it out with my aunt the other day because she said something about Daphne settling for the first girl that came along."

"I guess she has no idea Daphne dated before me. Oh well, I have my own crazy parents to deal with. Could you imagine if we *were* getting married? I'd shoot my damn self before I ever made it down the aisle."

Heather laughed.

"I just pulled up at the office. If you don't hear from me by Tuesday check the newspaper," Britton said.

"Want to meet for lunch later?"

Brides

"I'll try. Friday's are always crazy to begin with and I have potential client meetings, so I was planning a working lunch, but I'll see what I can do."

"Either way, let me know what happens with the King and Queen on Sunday."

Britton laughed and ended the call before getting out of the car. Her cell beeped, informing her of a new text message, so she checked it as she walked through the main doors.

I lost my panties in your apartment, Daphne texted.

Ok, she replied.

"Britton, would you mind stepping into my office?" Phil Mason, the main partner of the design firm asked as soon as she walked through the door.

"Sure, let me set my briefcase in my office and I'll be right there."

"There's no need for that," he said, nodding towards his office door.

Well, here we go, she thought as she followed him. At least he was firing her on a Friday. She'd have the weekend to stew on it and get her portfolio together before hitting the ground Monday to try and find a new job.

Britton sat in the chair across from his massive desk. Phil had always reminded her of a weasel. He was tall and skinny with large ears and beady eyes that were too close together. At the moment, she thought of him as a spineless weasel.

"As I'm sure you know, your temporary year has passed."

"Yes, I am aware," she replied, watching his face wrinkle as he tried to adjust with glasses with his nose. She was beyond pissed and her creative mind began morphing him into a cartoon weasel as he continued. She hadn't heard a word he'd said, until he finished and asked what her thoughts were.

"Phil, I've brought in four large projects and assisted on a half dozen others in the year that I've worked here. Honestly, I think I've done more work than your last three or four temp hires all together, from what I've been told. If my work is not up to your standard, you've never made mention of it." She watched his face distort as she continued. "I chose a temp position with this smaller company over an internship with a large corporation because I thought this was a company I could grow with. I guess I was mistaken." She stood with her hand out. "I expect a good reference from this company and I'd appreciate any recommendations you have on other companies."

"Britton, didn't you hear what I just said? You're not fired. I made you an offer to come join us as our lead architect," he said, finally pushing his glasses up where they belonged.

"You did?" She sat back down with a distant look on her face.

"Are you feeling okay?" he asked.

"Yes. I...I've had a lot going on lately and I wasn't expecting this. Lead architect?"

"You're very talented, Britton. I'd be a fool to let you go somewhere else." He handed her an envelope. "Here's the official employment offer with the figures and everything. Go ahead and take the rest of the weekend to think it over. We'll meet Monday, say eight a.m., to discuss it."

Britton stuffed the envelope into the side of her briefcase, but it wouldn't go all the way down in there. She pulled it back out and stuck her hand in there to see what was blocking it. Her heart skipped a beat and her eyes nearly bugged out of her head when her hand came in contact with lace material. She swallowed the lump in her throat and stuffed the envelope as far as it would go and shook his hand before leaving the small building.

As soon as she was in the car, Britton opened the envelope. The offer was a small six figure income with full benefits and bonus potential. It was what she'd expected, so she wasn't sure why she had such mixed feelings. It was too early to go have a drink, so she called Heather to make a lunch date and texted Daphne.

Found ur panties

Aren't u at the office? Where were they? Daphne replied.

Britton pushed the Bluetooth button and waited for the line to pick up.

"Hey," Daphne answered.

"They were in the side pocket of my briefcase. I couldn't figure out what was in there and almost pulled them out in front of Phil Mason."

"Oh shit," Daphne laughed. "Wait, why aren't you at work? Did he fire you?"

"No," she sighed. "He actually gave me an attractive offer to join the firm as the lead architect."

"Britton, that's great!"

"I know, I guess I was expecting him to fire me, so it hasn't really sunk in. He told me to take until Monday to get back to him."

"We should celebrate this weekend," Daphne said.

"I've been summoned to Sunday brunch."

"Uh-oh."

Britton laughed. "Heather said the same thing."

"I'm not sure if I like the fact that my cousin knows what's going in your life way before I do," Daphne chided.

"I'm sorry. I'm so used to talking to Heather about everything. I guess I'm still getting used to being in a real relationship."

"It probably doesn't help that we only see each other on the weekends and occasionally during the week," Daphne sighed. "When are you going to build your house?"

"I don't know. I have to re-draw most of the sketches. They got wet somehow. Any idea how that happened?" Britton teased.

"Nope," Daphne answered nonchalantly. "Speaking of something wet—"

"Stop, don't go there. I'm liable to drive off the damn road!"

Daphne laughed. "Hey, since you're not doing anything, do you want to come out here for lunch?"

"I can't. I already made plans with Heather."

Daphne huffed. "If she wasn't married and straight, I might have to claw her eyes out," she teased. "Dinner?"

"Yes."

Brides

"I'll try to leave a little early. Do you want to go somewhere or do you want me to cook for you?"

"If we don't go somewhere, we're liable to starve to death. You know we don't eat much food when we're together."

Daphne giggled. "Yes, we do seem to be occupied by other things. Maybe it's a good thing we live so far apart."

"Do you think the spark would die if we lived together?" Britton asked.

"No. That sparks been lit for over ten years. I doubt it's going anywhere. Why? Is Miss No Commitment ready to move in together?"

"Why does everyone call me that?"

"Have you met yourself?" Daphne retorted.

Britton's phone beeped with an incoming call. "Daph, I gotta go. My sister's calling. I wonder if she's going to brunch too. I'll see you tonight. I love you." She hung up and switched over.

"Bridget? What's up?"

"Mom mentioned something about checking the country club's booking schedule. Is there something you and Daphne haven't told me?"

"Nope," Britton sighed. "Why does everyone think we need to get married right now?" she growled.

"You two should at least be engaged. You've known each other forever and you're all Daphne talks about. I have to admit, it was odd at first, listening to her dote on you, but you're both so happy together."

"She does?"

"Oh my God, yes. It's like you pulled a Britton cap over her eyes and you're all she sees."

Britton laughed.

"I'd like my best friend back at some point, but I'd rather have her as a sister-in-law."

"Oh, for crying out loud with this marriage bullshit. I need to get off the phone. I'll see you Sunday at brunch."

"Wait!" Bridget yelled. "What brunch? Mom didn't mention that to me."

"That's odd."

"What did you do?"

"Nothing!" Britton shouted.

"I'll call mom and see if she forgot to mention it. Wade has golf plans with his manager. He's hoping for a promotion, but I can go to brunch."

"Well, technically, it was dad who summoned me, not mom. She may not even know about it."

"Is he still trying to change your mind?"

"Yes, even after I built that damn building for him to prove I'm great at what I do and I'm doing what I love. Anyway, this is my battle to hash out with him."

"Alright, well let me know what happens."

"I'm sure mom will tell you before I do. Tell Wade I said hey," Britton said, hanging up as she pulled into the parking lot of her apartment building.

Britton walked inside, tossing her briefcase on the coffee colored couch as she passed by on the way to her bedroom. She quickly changed from her pantsuit and dress boots to shorts, a sports bra, and a t-shirt. She laced up her sneakers and grabbed her keys as she headed out to the gym. She hadn't been in over a week and she had a lot of frustration to work out.

Brides

Chapter 4

Heather watched Britton walk from her car to the restaurant. She was fashionably late as usual and dressed casually in jeans, a canary yellow blouse with three-quarter sleeves and brown loafers with no socks. The buttons of her blouse were open to the top of her cleavage and a thin gold chain rested against her olive skin just below her collarbone. Her thick wavy hair fell loosely on her shoulders.

"You're sexy as hell, you know that? Oh, wait who am I kidding, you're Britton Prescott, of course you know it," Heather teased as Britton sat in the chair across from her.

"What's gotten into you?" Britton picked up the menu. "Should I be worried you're thinking of crossing over? Daphne mentioned something about us being too close and scratching your eyes out if you weren't straight."

Heather laughed. "Trust me, you might be oozing sex appeal, but I'm strictly dickly."

Britton's face wrinkled as she shrugged. "Hey, we both know you were dropped on your head as baby."

They laughed as the waitress came over to take their order.

"So, is the offer what you wanted?" Heather asked.

"Yes. I don't know why I'm hesitant. I guess I'm surprised. By the way, I talked to Bridget and apparently she's not invited to Sunday brunch."

Heather raised an eyebrow.

"More than likely, my dad plans to grill me again about coming over to the company. I'm over the whole damn thing and I'm ready to let him know that once and for all. Oh and to top it all off, Bridget said mom's looking at the country club's booking schedule. I seriously hope she's not planning my wedding when I'm not even fucking engaged. My parents are going to cause me to wind up in the looney bin."

Heather snickered.

"It's not funny. They can both kiss my ass."

"What are you and Daphne doing this weekend?"

"Same thing we do every weekend, have sex all over the apartment in every position we can get into," she answered nonchalantly.

"Seriously! I did not need to know that!"

"We'll you asked." Britton smiled.

"You two need to move in together."

"Don't start."

"Well, you do."

Britton raised an eyebrow.

"You know I want you to get married too, but I'd be happy if you at least moved in together. Hell, you live in different states."

"I've been thinking about the moving thing. I need to see what the hell my parents are up to and figure out if I'm going to take this job offer before I make any rash decisions about anything, including moving in together. I have so much on my plate right now; it's about to fucking fold in half."

Brides

"I think you need a girl's night out."

"Me too, but I honestly don't have time for that either." Britton took a long sip of her water, wishing it was wine. She watched the waitress place their lunch order on the table and walk away. Somehow, the arugula salad she'd ordered didn't look as appealing as it had sounded.

~

Britton and Daphne had spent most of Friday night and early Saturday morning wrapped in the sheets, which was why Britton was still asleep at ten in the morning.

"Wake up sleepyhead," Daphne whispered, brushing Britton's hair off her cheek. Her soft, naturally tanned skin contrasted against the crisp white bed linens.

"Go away," Britton grumbled.

"Aww, is that any way to treat the person who made you breakfast?" Daphne chided.

"Is there coffee?"

"Yes."

"I don't smell it."

Daphne laughed. "Get your lazy butt up and come eat. There's an entire pot of fresh coffee waiting for you."

Britton pried one gray eye open, then the other. Daphne tucked her chin length blond hair behind her ear as she bent down to kiss Britton's lips softly.

"Good morning."

"You said that to me hours ago as the sun came up while you were sitting—"

Daphne put her hand over Britton's mouth. "Go eat before it gets cold and I have to give it to the neighbor's cat."

"Cat? Wouldn't that be a dog you give scraps too?" Britton questioned as she sat up yawning. Daphne watched as the sheet fell below her nicely shaped round breasts.

"Huh?"

"Daph...eyes up here, babe," Britton teased. "The neighbor's cat..." she said with a little more enthusiasm.

Daphne rolled her eyes and walked across the room. "The older couple next door have this huge cat that looks like he belongs in a zoo. Anyway, a couple of years ago I saw him out back and thought he was a stray, so I gave him some bacon and eggs. It turned out that he was the neighbor's cat. He comes over every now and then for breakfast."

"I could easily insert a dirty comment here about you having breakfast with more than one feline, but I'll let it slide," Britton teased.

"Thank you so much for sparing me," Daphne laughed. "Get dressed, you're dangerous with no clothes on and I have things to do today," she said, walking out of the room.

A few minutes later, Britton walked into the kitchen. Daphne was leaning down, placing something in the refrigerator. Britton's mouth watered when she ran her eyes up Daphne's toned legs to the hint of ass cheeks peeking out from the bottom of her short shorts. She walked closer, pressing her crotch against Daphne's ass. Daphne stood up, leaning back against Britton as she pushed the refrigerator door closed.

Britton ran one hand up under Daphne's tank top, palming her naked breasts as her other hand slipped easily under the shorts, finding the wetness she knew was there. Daphne laid her head back against Britton's shoulder. Britton kissed the delicate skin of her neck as she rubbed her fingers back and forth.

Daphne moaned and rocked her ass against Britton's crotch as her body began to tremble with release. She'd woken up wanting more of the beautiful woman lying next to her, but her growling stomach had coaxed her out of bed. She ran her hand under Britton's hair to the back of her neck, and turned slightly to claim her lips in a passionate kiss as the last of the euphoria dissipated.

"God," Daphne panted, turning fully around in Britton's arms.

"Yes," Britton answered.

Daphne laughed and smacked her shoulder. "It's probably a good thing we don't live together. We'd probably die of sexual overload."

Britton grinned, kissing her lips once more. "You don't think we'd get sick of each other and experience lesbian bed death?"

"Is that really a thing?" Daphne asked, leaning back in her arms and looking into her eyes.

Britton shrugged. "I've never been in a long enough relationship to find out."

"Yeah, I've never lived with anyone I've dated either," Daphne replied, "But then again, none of my relationships have been like this either. I've never wanted someone so bad that I couldn't function."

"I can't say I have either. I mean hot sex is one thing, but physically aching for someone is something new to me too." Britton smiled. "I guess we can't move in together then, because I'd rather go on aching for you when I can't see you than be right next to you and not feel any want at all."

"I love you," Daphne said, kissing her deeply.

Britton's growling stomach grabbed their attention.

"I guess I'd better feed the beast," Daphne teased as she pulled away.

Britton washed her hands in the sink and sat down at the small round table. Daphne set a plate of warm pancakes and turkey bacon in front of her, along with a steaming cup of coffee, before sitting down next to her with her own plate and cup.

"You said you have plans today," Britton said between bites.

"Yeah, my mom's birthday is Monday, so I planned a girl's afternoon with her. We're going shopping and having lunch."

"Does she still think you need to date other people?"

"It's not necessarily other people. She likes you and your family. She just doesn't realize you're not my first girlfriend. I've tried to explain to her that I've dated…a lot, but I've loved you for years. There's a huge difference. She'll come around eventually. What about your mom?"

"What about her?" Britton mumbled with her mouth full of pancakes.

"You haven't talked about her much. Everything's been about your dad and the company building."

"Mom's focused on her latest endeavor," Britton sighed.

"Oh really? There's no stopping your mother when she gets something in her crosshairs," Britton laughed.

"Yeah, no kidding." Britton shook her head. "You're all she talked about at the unveiling."

Daphne smiled. "What can I say? I'm practically perfect."

Britton smiled, shaking her head.

Brides

Chapter 5

The rest of Saturday had gone by in a blur of music and chemicals as Britton caught up on her cleaning, scrubbing every inch of her apartment until it was spotless. Daphne had shown up with dinner and they'd spent another nearly sleepless night together.

Britton fumbled around half asleep trying to find her phone when it rang loudly at eight o'clock.

"Hello?" she yawned.

"I was calling to tell you good luck at brunch and call me as soon as it's over," Heather said.

"What time is it?"

"Eight."

"Fuck!" Britton yelled. "I have to be there at ten!"

"Are you still in bed?" Heather asked. "Let me guess, Daphne's there and you were up all night. You know what will solve this sex binge thing you two have going on."

"Heather, I don't have time for that right now. I'll call you later."

Daphne was sitting up in the middle of the bed with the sheets pooling around her waist. Britton felt the tinge of arousal when she saw Daphne's naked torso.

"Shoot me now and get it over with," Britton huffed. "Better yet, come with me. There's no way my parents will get into an argument with me in front of you." Britton smiled, biting her bottom lip.

"I love you, but no way. You're on your own with those two," Daphne laughed and laid back down. "Tell them I said hello," she yawned.

Britton showered almost too quickly to apply soap to her skin and toweled off in record time. Although she hated blow-drying her hair, she couldn't wait for it to air dry, so she dried it quickly and let it fall in natural waves over her shoulders.

"I swear I'm going to chop this shit off one day," she growled.

"No you're not!" Daphne interjected from under the covers.

"If you want long hair, grow yours out."

"I do let it grow a little longer sometimes to change it up, but I look ridiculous with hair as long as yours, so that's not happening."

"Don't ever cut yours any shorter then!" Britton replied, walking out of her closet in dark gray slacks and a thin purple v-neck sweater. She sat on the edge of the bed to zip up her ankle boots.

"You're beautiful," Daphne murmured.

"So you've said," Britton replied, leaning down to kiss her. "Have you looked in the mirror lately? You're adorable all snuggled up in my bed sheets. I wish I didn't have to leave you."

"Get going. You definitely don't want to be late."

"Will you be here when I get back?" Britton asked, kissing her lips.

"Maybe," she teased.

Britton leaned closer, kissing her passionately.

Brides

Daphne put her hand on Britton's chest above her breasts and pushed her back. "Get out of here," she laughed.

~

Britton pulled around the circular driveway and parked near the front doors of the large estate house. Her mother was sitting in the solarium, flipping through the pages of a magazine when Britton walked in.

"Hello, sweetheart. You look tired," her mother said when she hugged her.

"I haven't slept much this weekend," she answered honestly. "Is Daddy in his office?"

"Yes. Brunch will be served out here in half an hour."

Britton nodded and walked through the house to her father's study. Stephen Prescott was sitting in the high back leather chair behind his desk, looking out the window at the sprawling landscape.

"Hi, Daddy." Britton walked in and shut the door. Her father stood to hug her, then sat back in his chair.

"A few things have come to my attention recently. The first being that job of yours. I've taken the liberty to have a proposal drawn up for you." He opened the top drawer of his desk, removed a thick packet of papers, and slid it over to her. "I think you will see that this is an attractive offer."

"Daddy, I love what I do. I wish you would see that being an architect is what I want to do. I was offered a contract on Friday to join the firm as a lead architect. That kind of thing never happens to someone who isn't even two years out of college. I'm going to take their offer. I have no interest in working for the family business. I know that hurts your feelings and I'm sorry—"

"Britton," he sighed. "Look at the papers in front of you." He watched her pull the packet closer. "I know you don't want to work at Prescott's, but I also know you're wasting your talent away at that little bitty company you work for. This is a business proposal for you to start your own firm. I'll come in as a silent investor, funding the start-up and as soon as you're on your feet, it's all yours."

"What?" she questioned, flipping through the pages of the packet. "Daddy? Are you serious?"

He smiled. "Britton, you're a very talented woman. I wouldn't be any kind of father if I didn't encourage you to be the best in your field and do everything I could do to help you succeed."

"I don't know what to say." Britton looked at all of the zeros in the figure on the bank papers.

"Since you're not affiliated with Prescott's, you know Bridget will be my successor and thus, the company will be hers since it is privately held. However, you still have your inheritance from your grandfather that you receive monthly. This business deal has nothing to do with Prescott's. I had your name put on four of my CD's at the bank as an additional account holder."

"Are you sure you want to do this? I haven't been out of school long and out of the dozen projects I've worked on, I headed only four of them."

"Britton, any investment is a risk. Honestly, I'm not the one risking anything, it's you. This investment money is essentially a percentage of your inheritance up front that you would have received when I passed away. So, the question is, are you sure you want to do this?"

Brides

"I really don't know. I mean, sure I want my own firm, but I figured it would be years down the road," she said.

"I think you're wasting your time with that little firm, not to mention them leaving you dangling on a hook for two months wondering whether or not you will be employed from one day to the next. That's asinine and poor business practice if you ask me. You deserve better than that. You're a Prescott and that name goes a long way in this state as well as parts of New England in general. Don't you ever forget that."

"Yes, sir."

"I know I've given you a lot to think about and I don't expect an answer today. You have the papers. Take your time and look it all over."

"Okay." She rose from the chair across from his desk and walked around to hug him. "Thank you, Daddy."

"You're welcome."

Britton moved to walk out of the room, but he stopped her.

"I'm not finished," he said.

She sat back down.

"I've been talking to your mother and it seems something else is in order." He got up from his desk and walked over to the large painting on the wall, pushing it to the side to reveal the wall safe.

Britton raised an eyebrow and watched as he turned the dial and popped the door open. She'd only ever seen the safe being used three times in her life, once by her father and twice by her grandfather.

"You know when Bridget got married your mother gave Wade her engagement ring to propose to your sister with and well, I had this saved away for my son one day to give to his bride," he said, handing her an old velvet box.

Britton opened the box, revealing her grandmother's antique wedding ring. It was a large, princess cut, blue diamond, that was set in white gold, with small white diamonds surrounding the large blue one and continuing down the band on both sides.

"This is beautiful," she exclaimed.

"Your mother and I are both happy to see you settling down in a committed relationship and we would love none other than to have Daphne as a daughter-in-law. You're obviously very much in love with each other. I don't think I've ever seen you light up the way you do when she's around."

Britton stared at him like a deer in headlights. Her heart was racing so fast her lungs could barely keep up and she was on the verge of fainting.

"Anyway, this ring is yours now. I'm looking forward to seeing it on Daphne's hand."

Britton swallowed the lump in her throat and forced a smile as she closed the box and hugged him.

"Thank you," she finally said.

~

The rest of brunch with Britton's parents went rather well. No one spoke about the business deal or the ring and her mother only mentioned the word marriage twice. Britton barely ate because the butterflies in her stomach were threatening to break through the skin at any moment. So, she pushed her food around to make it look like she'd eaten the majority. She was thankful her

Brides

mother served bloody mary's, and even though she thought they were disgusting, she drank three of them.

As soon as she was in her car, she dialed Heather's number. She knew Daphne should be the first person she called, but she was in shock over the business deal and the ring and she didn't want to blurt out the wrong thing to Daphne.

"How'd it go?" Heather asked, noticing the name on her caller ID.

"If I smoked pot, I'd probably smoke an entire tree right now," Britton exclaimed.

Heather laughed. "What happened? And by the way, pot doesn't grow on trees. It's a plant."

"Fine. I'd light one end of the plant and smoke the whole damn thing."

Heather snickered. "It can't be that bad."

Britton huffed. "You have no idea."

"Come over. Greg's at his friend Joe's house, helping him build a deck for the new fire pit he just bought."

"I remember him from the bachelor party. Do the two of them even know how to build a deck?"

"I have no idea. They made a bunch of measurements last night and drew something on a piece of paper. Greg met him at the hardware store as soon as it opened this morning. I told him to call you. You know men and their manly things," she giggled sarcastically.

"I can only imagine how it will turn out," Britton laughed. "I'll be there in about twenty minutes. Get a bottle of wine ready," she said.

~

Britton bounced from foot to foot waiting for Heather to open the front door. She needed to calm her nerves before she had a stroke. Her mind was still reeling from the meeting with her father. Her own business sounded like a great idea, but it was also a huge risk going out on her own with very little experience. The ring was a whole different story. She reached down, touching the box in her pocket. Marriage was something Britton had never wanted for herself and the pressure to marry Daphne was overwhelming.

"Why didn't you use your key?" Heather chided, opening the front door.

It hadn't even dawned on Britton that she had a key. Her mind was on extreme overload.

"I don't know. I guess I forgot," she replied, walking inside. "Where's the wine?"

"I thought you were kidding."

"Do I look like I'm kidding?" Britton sighed as she flopped down on the couch.

"It can't be that bad. Is he forcing you to join the company? I know you said he was threatening your inheritance," Heather said, sitting next to her.

Britton laughed sarcastically. "I wish it were that easy."

Heather raised an eyebrow.

"He gave me access to part of my inheritance to start my own firm with him as a silent investor. Once the firm takes off, he will withdraw his investment and I will be the sole owner."

"Wow! That's...incredible, Britton."

"Yeah," Britton exhaled deeply. "It's a huge risk though. The firm finally made me an offer to join them permanently as a lead architect. I don't know what to do."

Brides

"I would think your own business would be a lot better than working for someone else."

"That's true, but I don't have a lot of experience and that could hurt me if I'm on my own. At least, under another company I'll have their name and experience to back me up."

"It sounds like a huge decision. I can't believe he gave up on you joining his company."

"I guess he finally opened his eyes when I designed his new office building. I still think it was a huge test that I was supposed to fail," she replied with a shrug.

"What did Daphne say?"

"I haven't talked to her yet."

"She's going to be pissed that you told me first." Heather shook her head.

Britton pulled the box out of her pocket and set it on the coffee table in front of them.

"What's that?" Heather asked.

"The main reason I'm here," Britton sighed.

Heather gasped when she opened the box and saw the large glimmering ring. "What the hell?" she said.

"It was my grandmother's. My father gave it to me and basically told me to put it on Daphne's hand."

"Holy shit!"

"Yeah, no kidding."

"It's gorgeous, but is this really what you want?"

"I don't know. I love her and I can see spending the rest of my life with her. We have a lot of fun together, but—"

"You don't want to get married," Heather interjected.

"Exactly."

"What are you going to do?" Heather asked. "I mean, it is the natural next step, but if there is one thing I know about you, Britton, you don't do anything that's expected of you. Maybe this is the time to make an exception to your rule." she shrugged.

"You think I should marry her?"

"Well, you know I'm going to say yes. You're great together. I've never seen you this happy and she's my cousin, so we'd officially be related." Heather smiled, setting the box back on the table.

Britton stared at the box. Her head pounded the steady staccato of a stress headache.

"We don't even live together. Hell, we don't even talk about living together or getting married for that matter."

"Did your dad give you a timeframe?"

"No. I wouldn't have accepted the ring if he had. He made it pretty clear he expected it though. At least, my inheritance or the business deal weren't involved in that conversation. He's not going to force me to marry anyone. I think this is my mother's doing. She's already trying to book the country club for God's sake."

Heather raised her eyebrows and shook her head. "You're my best friend and she's my cousin. I can't tell you what to do, but I think everyone is expecting it."

"Maybe we could have a long engagement, say four or five years," Britton said seriously.

Heather laughed. "Try two years tops and with your mother, a year is too long."

Britton sighed. "I know. As soon as I put the ring on Daphne's hand my mother will have the wedding planned and the invitations out. She'll just give me a day and time to show up."

Heather giggled even though she knew her friend was being serious. "Hon, the best thing I can tell you is, do what you feel in your heart and to hell with everyone

Brides

else. It's your life. You know better than anyone what you want and how you see your future. If you want to have your own business, go for it and if you want to be with Daphne for the rest of your life, marry the damn girl and get it over with."

"I guess I have a lot to think about and I need to call her. I'm sure she's waiting to see how it went." Britton hugged her best friend before standing up. "Keep this between us. I'm not sure what I'm going to do yet, with either issue."

"Your secret is safe with me, but if you propose, I better be the first person you tell," Heather teased.

"You may need to be there in case of emergency. I'm liable to have a stroke," Britton laughed.

~

Daphne's Mercedes was still in the parking lot when Britton returned home. She put the ring in her car's glove compartment and locked it with her key, before going inside. Daphne was sitting on the couch in a thin pair of cotton pants and a t-shirt, watching a movie on the TV. Britton glanced at the screen, nearly fainting when she saw the bride walking down the aisle.

"I was beginning to wonder if you were still alive," Daphne teased, leaning over to kiss Britton softly when she sat down next to her.

Britton pulled Daphne into her lap, wrapping her arms around her as she laid her head on her shoulder. "What are you watching?"

"I don't know. It's some kind of romance movie marathon. This is the sequel to the movie that just finished."

"Must be in the air," Britton muttered under her breath.

"Huh?"

"Do you see yourself doing that?" Britton nodded towards the TV.

Daphne turned her eyes to the TV, then back to Britton. "Getting married? Yes, of course. What girl doesn't?"

Britton looked away from Daphne and nuzzled her head near the crook of her neck. Daphne backed away slightly to see her face again.

"What happened at your parents' house?" she asked curiously.

"I wish you'd gone with me," she sighed.

"Was it that bad?" Daphne asked, running her hand through Britton's long hair.

"My father released some of my inheritance money to me to start my own design firm with him as a silent investor until it gets off the ground."

"Whoa, I wasn't expecting that." Daphne leaned back, slightly shocked. "I thought he wanted you to join the company?"

"I guess he finally realized it wasn't going to happen."

"What are you going to do?"

"I don't know. It's a huge risk. I'd be using a good sized chunk of my inheritance to fund it and then basically rolling the dice."

"Is he going to be a silent partner?"

"Something like that, or at least a silent investor. Obviously, Bridget has the family business coming to her. I guess this is his way of doing something for me. I can't even think right now. My head is going in a hundred different directions."

"You're an amazing architect. You certainly have the talent and the business sense to own your own firm, but I know you're leery about your experience level. Whatever you decide, I'm behind you one hundred percent. I love you, Britton. Win or lose, I'd bet on you every time. I'm not with you for your money."

"That's good to know because if I do this and it fails, I won't have much of it," she laughed and kissed her softly, lingering near her lips before kissing her harder. "I love you and I can think of a lot of other things we could be doing right now than watching some wedding move."

"Oh really?"

Britton pushed Daphne to the side and crawled on top of her. "Oh yes."

"There's no better way to spend a Sunday afternoon than in your arms," she said, pulling Britton down for a searing kiss.

Chapter 6

Two weeks later, Britton signed the lease on a small office building in the middle of town. She'd already drawn out her interior changes and had a construction crew scheduled to incorporate those changes. The sign company was also scheduled. By the end of the week, Prescott Designs would be up and running. She had all of her permits in her hand and a smile on her face. Her dream had come true a little sooner than expected and she was as nervous as a mouse in a room full of traps, but she was excited to be starting a new venture. Phil Mason was sorry that she'd refused his offer and very unhappy about having her as his competition, but he'd told her he knew she was going to be a big name one day when he'd seen her first sketch.

She waited for her new landlord to drive away before pushing the button to call the person at the top of the favorites list in her phone. It rang twice before she heard the sweet voice that made her stomach flip flop.

"Hey, babe. Is it done?" Daphne asked.

"Yep. I'm officially a business owner."

"I wish I could've been there. I'm so happy for you."

"Thanks. It was easier than I anticipated. The crew will be here tomorrow to build out the interior and the signs should be up before the weekend."

Brides

"I hate that we live so far apart. We should go out tonight to celebrate."

"Yeah, I was thinking the same thing. I have to meet the construction crew pretty early though. Why don't we celebrate this weekend?"

"Great idea. I love you, Britton."

"I love you too. I better go call Heather. She's left two voicemails." Britton laughed and hung up the phone, before pushing the next name on the favorites list.

"Well?" Heather asked, answering the phone.

"It's official."

"Awesome! I'm so happy for you."

"Thanks. I'm scared to death, but I'm sure everything will be fine."

"We need to celebrate."

"You sound like your cousin."

Heather laughed. "It's good to know you called her before me this time. So, when's the celebration?"

"This weekend. I'm too busy to drive out to her place and she has meetings."

"That means you'll be celebrating between the sheets," Heather teased. "When are you two going to move in together? I'm afraid you're both going to spontaneously combust before you make it to one of your sex-filled weekends."

Britton laughed. "We haven't really talked about it."

"What about that other thing?" Heather asked.

"What thing?"

"The little box burning a hole in the back of your mind."

Britton laughed. "What about it?"

"Is there any upcoming news I need to be prepared for?"

"Nope."

"I take it you haven't talked to your mother," Heather laughed.

"Nope," Britton laughed too. "I've talked to my father about the business. Since he's an investor I have to let him know every time I do something financially, but he hasn't mentioned it."

"How long will he be an investor?"

"Until the company makes enough money to cover his investment and return rate. His rate is low, so I'd say two or three years probably."

"See, if you get engaged now, you have an excuse for a long engagement."

"Uh huh," Britton laughed. "Maybe I should start hounding you about kids the way you hound me about getting married."

"Oh God, I'm not having kids right now. My mom's already started asking when she's going to have grandkids."

"I'm sure my mother is hounding my sister too. I stay away from the two of them when they're together. They drive me nuts."

Heather laughed. "I have a patient coming in. I'll call you tonight. Maybe we can grab a glass of wine."

"Sounds good," Britton said, hanging up. She locked the door to the small office building and headed to the craft store to pick up the materials she'd ordered before heading home to start building the model for her next project.

~

Brides

Three weeks later, the construction was finished and the decorators had come and gone. The doors to Prescott Designs were open and the phones were ringing. Britton was in the process of trying to hire a secretary for the front desk and a design assistant. She'd already had two inquiries to bid on upcoming projects, one of which was a small waterfront bar and night club and she'd won the bid for a new library in one of the smaller nearby cities.

Britton pulled up at Daphne's townhouse and was surprised when she walked outside before Britton could get out of the car. Britton met her in the driveway.

"You look happy about something," Britton said, kissing her softly.

"I missed you and I have some interesting news to tell you."

"Do you want to stay in?" Britton raised an eyebrow.

"No. You said you were taking me somewhere for a nice romantic dinner and as much as I'd love to go inside right now and peel you out of that business suit, one seductive layer at a time, I'm done eating cardboard take out every weekend. Now, let's go," she chided, smacking Britton on the butt.

"Did you seriously just smack my ass?" Britton shrieked.

Daphne laughed and slid down into the passenger seat of Britton's sports car.

"I can't believe you. What if your neighbors saw that?" Britton shook her head.

Daphne shrugged. "They could use a little spice in their lives if you ask me."

"Spice?! Who are you and what have you done with my girlfriend?"

"Not seeing you all week makes me spicy I guess," Daphne teased.

"Are you sure you want to go—"

"Britton Prescott, you better drive this car before I do it for you."

Britton smiled and drove towards the interstate.

"Where are we going?" Daphne asked.

"It's a secret." Britton grinned.

"I could've met you at your apartment," Daphne said, realizing they were headed towards Providence. "You didn't have to drive all the way out to get me."

"It's fine, besides, we're going to a few places."

"We are?"

"Yes, so sit back and ride," Britton said, changing lanes and accelerating past a slower car.

"Oh, I'd like to sit back and ride right now," Daphne whispered in a seductive tone, causing Britton to grind the gears.

"You're trouble," Britton smiled, shaking her head.

"How so? You're the one who can't seem to handle the stick," she teased.

"I'll handle the stick alright," Britton laughed. "What am I going to do with you?"

"I don't know, but I'm looking forward to it."

"I'm beginning to think Heather's right," Britton murmured.

"Heather? Right about what?"

"Something stupid she said the other day about catching fire?"

"That was a good movie," Daphne replied.

"Huh?"

"Catching Fire. Did you see it?"

Brides

"No. I barely have time to eat, much less watch movies. All of my free time is spent with you."

"It's the sequel to Hunger Games. We saw that...or parts of it at least."

"Oh, I remember that. We were too busy with our own hunger games," Britton laughed.

"Yeah, and lately, all we've been doing is catching fire," Daphne grinned.

"Somehow, I don't think they had us in mind when they made those movies, but it sure sounds like it."

"There's a third one. I haven't seen it yet though."

"What's it called? Maximum Climax?"

Daphne laughed. "No, it's called Mockingjay."

"What the hell?" Britton furled her eyebrows.

"If you'd read the books or actually watched the movies, you'd understand what it is."

"I'll take your word for it," Britton said, merging onto a different interstate. "It sounds like lesbian bed death. First, you meet and you have Hunger Games, then you start dating and it's Catching Fire, then you move in together and it's Mockingjay, as in To Kill a Mocking Bird."

Daphne laughed. "Where are you going?"

"We're almost there," Britton replied.

Daphne stared out the window, watching the signs go by. As soon as they entered the Warwick city limits, Britton got off the interstate. She'd only been to Warwick a few times, but the small city was quiet with very little crime. They turned down a road with neighborhoods on both sides.

"Are we going to someone's house?" Daphne asked.

Britton pulled up in front of a beautiful beachfront house on Buttonwoods Beach at the very end of the road on the right side, and cut off the engine. It was a little smaller than her parents' estate house in Newport.

"Come on," she said, nodding towards the door for Daphne to get out.

Britton grabbed her hand and walked across the street to a clearing between the trees. The houses on this side of the street were all waterfront on Buttonwoods Cove. The last two lots on the cove side of the street were vacant and secluded with a large beach next door that formed the tip where the cove and ocean met.

"Have you ever been here?" Britton asked.

"No, but it's absolutely beautiful. Do you know the people who live across the street?"

"I've talked to them a couple of times. They're an older couple who have lived here a long time. They raised their four children in that house, all of whom have grown up and return on the holidays with their own children. The house next door to these two vacant lots is a retired couple whose children are in college. They travel a lot and are rarely home.

Daphne nodded. "You know a lot about the people who live around here," she murmured, looking back at the cove in front of them. She noticed something closer to the water and walked down towards it. Britton walked next to her. As they got closer, Daphne realized it was a large model of a two story house, sitting on a table that was covered with a dark tablecloth.

"Is this your newest design?" Daphne asked.

Britton nodded. "It's actually going right here where we are standing on both of these lots. It will be private and gated with its own beach and a large boat dock."

Brides

"Oh my, it's beautiful, Britton," Daphne said, walking around the table, looking at the model of the large house from all sides.

Britton pulled the front of the model open, revealing the layout. Daphne stepped closer, looking at the large spiral staircase in the center. The kitchen and family room were in the back with a solarium off of them. A formal living room was in the front and there were a couple of bedrooms on the first floor and a couple more on the second floor.

"This is amazing, Britton. Did you design the entire thing or did the owners tell you what they wanted?"

"This is all my design from the ground up, including the landscaping."

"You're so damn creative."

"The master bedroom is on the second floor and runs along the back where this balcony is here, overlooking the cove," Britton pointed out.

"Wow, what a view to wake up to," Daphne replied, looking across the cove at the wooded area and beach on the opposite side and a good distance away.

Britton removed a small black box from her pocket. Daphne raised an eyebrow as Britton bent down on one knee.

"Daphne Atwood, I love you with all of my heart and I want to wake up to this view next to you for the rest of my life," Britton paused. Her hands trembled as she opened the box to reveal the glimmering blue diamond surrounded by white diamonds. "Will you marry me?"

Tears poured down Daphne's cheeks. She let them fall as she placed her hand on the side of Britton's face, smiling down at her. "Of course I want to spend the rest of my life with you. I love you more than anything in this world, Britton."

"So, is that a yes?" Britton wiped away her own tears.

"Yes! Yes! Yes!" Daphne shrieked.

Britton slide the ring onto her finger and stood, picking Daphne up off the ground in the process and kissing her hard. They kissed each other until they could no longer breathe. Britton gasped for air as she wiped the happy tears from Daphne's cheeks with one hand and kept the other arm wrapped around her waist.

"Is this real? All of this?" Daphne was overwhelmed.

"Yes. I've owned the land for a few years now. My grandparents owned it and gave it to me in their will. They owned property all over the state. I've been working on the perfect house for this spot every since the first time I drove out here to see it. I finally finished the design recently and the permits came through yesterday. The construction crew breaks ground in two weeks."

"Wow! This is..." She looked at the large ring glistening in the sun on her left hand. "I'm at a loss for words. Britton, I never knew I could love someone so much that it literally hurts. We could live in a cardboard box and that ring could be a plastic one you got from a quarter machine and I'd still love you just as much as I do right now."

"I feel the same way. You make me so happy. My days revolve around talking to you and counting the time until I see you again." Britton kissed her once more, before pulling away. She bent down, pulling a blanket, a bucket of ice with a chilled bottle of champagne in it, and two glasses from under the table.

Brides

"When did you have time to do all of this?" Daphne asked, sitting next to her on the blanket.

"I know the neighbors, remember." Britton smiled. "Mr. and Mrs. Lundy across the street saw me out here with the zoning people and came out to talk to me. I told them I was finally building and one thing led to another and I brought everything out here earlier and asked them to bring the chilled champagne over about twenty minutes before our arrival."

"What if I'd wanted to stay in and catch fire, as you suggested?" Daphne teased.

"Well, I guess they would've drank the champagne," she laughed. "I knew you really wanted to go somewhere tonight, so I was pretty sure you weren't going to stay in. Here's to spending the rest of our lives right here in this very spot," Britton toasted.

Daphne clinked her glass to Britton's. "I love you so damn much."

"I love you too." Britton smiled, wrapping her arm around her and squeezing her close.

Daphne sighed when she looked down at the ring on her finger.

"Do you like it?" Britton asked.

"Oh yes, it's…it's gorgeous. I'm going to be scared of something happening to it for the rest of my life," she said honestly.

"Don't worry, it's insured. Besides, it was my grandmother's and it's older than both of us and it's lasted this long. I'm sure it will outlive both of us too."

"Wow. Are you sure you don't want to wear it? Or maybe Bridget? Since it's a family heirloom."

"Nope. My dad gave it to me for you. Bridget has our mother's engagement ring. My parents gave it to

Wade when he was purposing. This ring was supposed to go to their son to propose with."

"So your parents already know?" Daphne asked.

"No. No one knows. Not even Heather," Britton smiled. "My dad gave it to me a while back for whenever I was ready. We don't have to tell anyone right away and a long engagement is fine with me."

"My parents are going to flip out, but I think everyone else will be happy for us. I plan on telling the world, right after we get out of here so I can get you naked and wet first, of course." Daphne grinned.

Britton smiled. "Yeah, I guess the middle of a neighborhood wasn't the best place to propose."

"Are you kidding, this was beautiful, Britton. I can't wait to live right here with you as your wife."

They walked back towards the car, leaving everything behind.

"Aren't we taking that with us?" Daphne asked.

"No. Mr. Lundy will get it and store it for me. I'll swing by next week and get it from him."

"Wow. So they just watched all of this from their house?"

Britton laughed. "No. They were going to play bridge with their friends and put the champagne out before they left. He said they wouldn't be home for a couple of hours. He thought I was just surprising you with finally building the house. They're both very nice. You'll like them. Everyone here is quiet and keeps to themselves," she said, closing Daphne's door and walking around to the driver's side. "Where do you want to eat?" she asked, starting the engine.

"Are you serious?"

Britton raised an eyebrow and looked over at her.

Brides

"All I want to do is get naked with you, so you better take me to your apartment before we get naked right here in front of Mr. Lundy's house."

Britton laughed and put the car in gear.

"What kind of wedding do you want?" Daphne asked, clicking her seatbelt.

"I haven't thought that far ahead, but I'm not a big flashy person, so maybe something small and less formal."

"Yeah, a nice intimate ceremony near the water would be beautiful," Daphne said.

Chapter 7

"I feel like a kept woman," Daphne laughed.

"Why is that?" Britton asked, driving her back to her house after spending the rest of the weekend wrapped in each other's arms.

"You picked me up Friday night and here you are driving me back home Sunday night."

"That's true, but there's one definite change," Britton said, running her hand over Daphne's left hand.

"I can't believe we went all weekend and didn't tell anyone. It reminds me of our sneaking around when we first got together."

"We are pretty good at keeping secrets. Maybe we should just elope." Britton shrugged.

"Your mother would strangle you, besides, I'm only doing this once and I want to do it right the first time."

"Do you remember what Heather and Bridget went through?" Britton reminded her. "It wasn't exactly a cake walk."

Daphne laughed.

"Hey, didn't you have something you wanted to tell me?" Britton asked as she merged onto the interstate.

"It's nothing major. You know how we just finished our semi-annual inventory and production assessment? My distribution center scored the highest."

Brides

"Wow, that's great, babe, especially now. Could you imagine if yours had scored the lowest?" Britton teased.

"Oh please, your parents love me and your dad respects me as one of his best employees."

"Yes, I know. I hear all the time how wonderful you are," Britton said. "I didn't join the family business, but they made sure I married into it," she whispered to herself as she pulled into Daphne's driveway.

"I hate leaving you," Daphne sighed.

"I know, me too." Britton kissed her softly. "You said it yourself, we haven't told anyone, which is fine with me, but I know you're itching to call my sister."

"Like you're not waiting to call my cousin!" Daphne chided as she got out of the car.

Britton shrugged. "I'm having lunch with her tomorrow. I might mention it in conversation," she grinned.

"Uh huh. The two of you can't keep anything from each other. You've always been attached at the hip. It used to drive me crazy."

"And now?" she asked, following Daphne into her townhouse.

Daphne grinned. "You can talk to her all you want, as long as I'm the only one lying naked and wet in your bed."

"You will definitely never find Heather in my bed…well there was that one time…but I doubt it will happen ever again. It wasn't exactly a great time," Britton teased.

"Oh gross, you slept with my cousin!"

"No," Britton laughed. "She passed out drunk in my bed. I found her naked and drooling all over my pillow the next morning."

Daphne laughed.

"On a serious note, will you give me time to tell my parents before you tell Bridget? I want them to hear it from me first."

"Sure. She's already going to be pissed that I waited all weekend to tell her, why not wait another hour."

"Hour?!"

"Yeah," Daphne paused, looking over at her. "You are telling them today, right?"

"I…"

"How about we tell everyone together?"

"You want to have an engagement party?" Britton raised an eyebrow.

"No," Daphne laughed. "Let's call everyone together. We can start with your parents and then Bridget and Heather."

"What about your parents?"

Daphne bit her bottom lip in thought. "I'm debating whether to tell them in person or just call them. What about your parents? Do you think calling them is okay?"

Britton knew Daphne had no idea how strongly her parents felt about them getting married. She put her arm around Daphne and answered honestly.

"I think my parents love you more than me sometimes. I'm sure they will be disappointed we aren't there in person, but at the same time, they will be ecstatic to hear the news either way."

"Why do my parents have to be so difficult?" Daphne sighed, cuddling closer to Britton.

"I'm don't know, babe. We love each other and personally, I think that's all that matters."

"You're right. Let's get this over with," Daphne said, pushing off of her to grab her phone.

Brides

~

Daphne's parents sounded surprised and Britton was sure the news hadn't really sunk in with them as Daphne hung up the phone.

"Are you sure those were my parents?" she laughed.

"I guess they are coming around, finally."

"Britton, they've always liked you, but my mother can't comprehend that you're not the first girl I ever dated. I'm sure the other shoe will drop before it's over."

"Shall I explain to her how experienced you are in the lesbian department?" Britton raised an eyebrow. "Here, hand me the phone and I'll call her back."

Daphne laughed, snatching her phone away from Britton. "Don't you dare. She'd probably have a damn stroke if you start talking about sex with her."

Britton giggled.

"Okay, moving on to your parents," Daphne said, handing Britton's phone to her.

Britton scrolled through her contacts to her mother's cell phone and waited.

"Hello, darling," Sharon Prescott answered.

"Hi, Mom. Is Daddy around?"

"He's in the study, reading some new bestselling book he picked up while we were out in the shops this morning. Why didn't you call his phone?"

"I wanted to talk to both of you. Can you go find him, please?"

"Yes, hold on."

Britton rolled her eyes and Daphne snickered when they heard her parents talking in muffled voices. Finally, the speakerphone came on.

"We're here," her mother said.

"I'm sorry to do this over the phone, but I, or rather we, wanted to be the first to tell you…"

Daphne leaned closer and she and Britton said together, "We're engaged!"

"Oh, that's wonderful news!" Sharon exclaimed.

"Congratulations to you both," her father stated. "Welcome to the family."

"Thank you," Daphne replied.

"Daphne you've always been a part of our family, but this makes it official. I'm so happy for you both."

"Thank you," Britton said. "We better go. Daphne's itching to call Bridget."

Everyone laughed and Britton hung up the phone. Daphne quickly dialed Bridget's number and got her voicemail, so she left her a quick message to her call her back as soon as possible, that she had something important to tell her.

"I guess this leaves Heather," Britton announced as she pushed the favorites button on her phone.

Heather answered on the second ring. "I'm surprised you came up for air. This must be an important call," she laughed.

"Ha-ha-ha, smartass. Daphne and I have some news to share with you," Britton replied.

"We're engaged!" they yelled together.

"Oh my God, you actually did it! That's great!"

"Thanks," Britton said.

"How do you like that ring, Daph? Isn't it gorgeous?" Heather asked.

Daphne looked at the phone, then back at Britton. "You showed her the ring?"

Brides

"She loves it," Britton responded. "I'll see you tomorrow."

"Sounds good. My love to you both," Heather said as she hung up.

Daphne's brow was furled as she waited.

"Yes. I was nervous. My father had just given it to me, along with the keys to my own company. I didn't know what to do, so I stopped by to see her. She's my best friend."

"Britton, what the hell? I cannot believe Heather not only knew about the proposal and saw my ring, but she also knew about your father's offer before I did. Are you kidding me with this? Don't you think those are things we should be sharing together?"

"I…"

"I'm your girlfriend and you want me to be your wife. Then, I should be your best friend. If I'm not the first person you want to tell everything to, then why the hell are we getting married?"

"Of course I want to tell you everything," Britton sighed. "Are we having our first official fight?" she asked.

"I don't know what it is, but right now, I think I really want to be alone. I'm not exactly feeling blissful anymore."

Britton stood up and walked to the door. "For what it's worth, I'm sorry," she said as she walked out.

Chapter 8

Britton's phone rang as she pulled into the parking lot. She saw her mother's face on the caller ID and decided now wasn't the time to talk to her, so she sent the call to voicemail. As soon as she found an open space to park in, her phone beeped with the message. She turned the car off and pushed the button to listen to the message.

Britton, it's your mother. I picked up the latest country club schedule this morning. We need to go over it as soon as possible. We have a little leeway since we're high priority, but we can't wait much longer. Call me when you get this. Oh and don't forget the costume party. Love you.

Britton tossed her phone into the passenger seat and walked into the restaurant, late as usual. Her demeanor was slightly off key as she meandered inside and slid into the bench across from Heather. The last thing she wanted to be doing was planning a wedding. The construction company had called her early that morning to talk about moving up the date to break ground on her house and she needed to schedule the final interviews for the handful of people who were candidates for the positions she needed to fill at her company. Not to mention, she also had a few bids to write in hopes of picking up some new business.

"You look tired," Heather said.

Brides

"I'm exhausted. I didn't sleep last night," Britton replied, ordering a water with lemon from the waitress.

"Now that you're getting married, maybe you two should start talking about moving in together."

"I don't think that's happening," Britton yawned.

"You're not going to live together?" Heather raised an eyebrow.

"Not getting married."

"What?"

"I'm pretty sure we had our first fight last night, or at least Daphne did."

"Well? What happened?"

"She didn't know you knew about the offer from my dad or the ring. She was beyond pissed that you saw it first. She said she should be the first person I want to share things with."

"She's right, you know. That's what marriage is about, equal partnerships and all of that other crap. The difference is, you're with another woman and women are needy. You and I are best friends and yes, there are things I tell you before I tell Greg, and things you know that I'll probably never tell Greg, but that's what best friends are for. Women tell each other everything and share everything. That's why it's not a problem in a regular marriage when a wife tells her best friend stuff before her husband."

"I'm so used to going to you with everything. Hell, we've been friends since we were kids. This entire thing is stupid."

"If you want to spend the rest of your life with her, you have to let her fill my shoes. I love you both and I want to see you both happy. You make each other happy, don't let something this stupid get in the way of that. You and I will always be best friends, Brit, but she's going to be your wife. In other words, the shit just got real."

Britton laughed. "Yeah, you're definitely right about that. Who knew a ring would come with a whole new set of rules," she said, shaking her head.

"No kidding. The whole ball and chain thing makes more sense to me now," Heather laughed.

Britton smiled and shook her head. "By the way, my mom left me a voicemail a little bit ago to give me the dates the country club has open on their schedule."

"No she didn't?" Heather snickered.

"Oh yes, she did. I don't even know if I'm still engaged and she's already got the date set, flowers order, pastor scheduled, and has the marriage certificate ready to sign."

Heather laughed hysterically. "I do not envy you."

"Shut up," Britton replied, shaking her head.

"I honestly never thought you'd do it…get married, I mean. I'm glad you're getting married, don't get me wrong, but I just never thought it would happen. You really love Daphne a lot to go through all of this."

"Actually, she's just really great in bed and great sex is what makes life worth living," Britton answered nonchalantly.

Heather shook her head. "You sound like a man."

"She is phenomenal in bed, but yes, you're right, I do love her. More than I ever thought I could love someone, to be honest with you."

"Then why are you sitting here telling me this? You need to go fix the train you derailed and tell that girl how much you love her. I'll always be your best friend, Britton, but Daphne will be your wife. Remember that."

Brides

"What would I do without you?" Britton said, sliding out of the bench and hugging Heather.

"Do you really want me to answer that?" Heather raised an eyebrow.

Britton laughed as she walked away.

~

The drive out to New Bedford gave Britton time to clear her head. It was getting too cool to ride with the top down in October, but the blaring radio helped to clear the cobwebs from her sleep deprived brain. She pulled into the parking lot for the Prescott's distribution center and parked in a front parking space. She pushed the sleeves of her sweater back on her forearms and checked herself in the mirror as she ran her fingers through her long hair. It settled around her shoulders in loose waves. She stuffed her keys into the pocket of her jeans and walked through the main doors. She didn't have security clearance to get upstairs since she wasn't an employee, so she stepped up to the front desk.

"I'd like to see Daphne Atwood, please."

"Who are you with?" The man behind the desk asked.

"With?"

"What company?"

"Oh, sorry, I'm not here on business. Can you tell her Britton Prescott's here to see her please?"

The man straightened his back, as if Britton's father had just walked through the door, and quickly dialed Daphne's extension. When she didn't answer, he called over the intercom that she had a guest in the lobby.

Britton leaned against the wall with her hands in her pockets. She'd never been to the New Bedford Distribution Center, but it looked similar to the others her father and grandfather had taken her to as a child and teenager.

Daphne stepped off the stairs and pushed the glass security door open.

"Hey," she said, smiling as she tucked her blond hair behind her ear out of habit.

Britton nodded towards the front doors and held one open as Daphne passed through. She leaned her back against her car door and noticed Daphne was still wearing her ring.

"I'm sorry. You should've been the first person to see that ring and I know I should've told you about my dad's business offer before anyone else. I'm still getting used to you being the top priority in my life. When I dated other people…I never put them above Heather in the chain of my life. She was always the first person I thought of telling something or showing something to."

Daphne opened her mouth to speak, but Britton held her hand up to stop her.

"Let me finish. Daphne, everything changed when we got together. I fell in love for the first time in my life. You're the first person I think of for everything and I'm still trying to get used to that."

"Britton, I know you and Heather are very close and honestly, I'm a little jealous of that. I'm sorry, I know it's stupid. I have a best friend too, but you're so much more than that to me. I don't want to be the jealous wife that looks over your shoulder all the time. I trust you and I have to learn to trust that you will share things with me when you're ready."

Brides

"Even though we've known each other for years, I guess there's still a lot to learn," Britton looked down at Daphne's hand. "I'm glad you're still wearing that."

Daphne raise an eyebrow. "Did you think I didn't want to marry you because I got mad about something? Britton, we're going to disagree and get mad, and probably argue and fight at some point, but that's part of being in a relationship. I love you and nothing will ever change that."

"I love you too," Britton said, pulling her close and kissing her tenderly.

Daphne wrapped her arms around Britton's neck, pushing her long hair back off her shoulders as Britton wrapped her arms around Daphne's waist, rocking their hips together.

"Do you know what the best part of all of this is?" Daphne asked breathlessly.

"Hmm?" Britton mumbled, kissing her neck.

"Make up sex." Daphne grinned.

"Oh, definitely yes." Britton moved back up, kissing her passionately.

Daphne moved her hands to Britton's chest above her breasts, pushing back to break the heated kiss.

"The entire building is probably watching us," she panted.

Britton moved her hand down to Daphne's ass, squeezing it through the dress slacks she was wearing.

"Britton!" she squealed, smacking her shoulder.

Britton shrugged with a grin. "If they're going to look, what not give them something to look at?"

"Uh huh," Daphne murmured, shaking her head. "You're trouble."

"But you love me." Britton smiled brightly.

"Yes…yes, I do." Daphne smiled back. Checking her watch, she said, "How long are you here for?"

"I don't know, maybe a little longer," Britton answered. "Why?"

"I can maybe be persuaded to take off a little early," Daphne said nonchalantly.

"Persuaded, huh," Britton laughed, pulling her back for another deep kiss. Then, slid her lips to Daphne's ear as she rubbed her crotch against Daphne's. "How's that?" she asked.

Daphne swallowed hard, trying to calm the butterflies in her stomach as her pulse raced. "Good," she whispered huskily.

Britton bit her bottom lip seductively and grinned.

Daphne felt like her libido had been slapped across the face and was now wide awake and ready for action.

"I can't go back to work like this." Daphne shook her head.

"Like what?"

"You know what. I'm so wet I can barely walk."

Britton laughed sympathetically.

"How are we ever going to live together? We're liable to kill each with our sex drives."

Britton smiled. "Nah, Mockingjay, remember. Our sheets will probably be cold."

Daphne laughed hysterically. "You're a mess."

"Actually, you are at the moment."

"Ass!" Daphne smiled, shaking her head.

"Hey, speaking of moving in together, they are breaking ground on the house this Friday instead of next Wednesday."

"Why is that?"

Brides

"I don't know. Something to do with the permits for another job."

"Friday is Halloween."

"Don't tell me you're superstitious. The last thing I need is a damn ghost in our house." Britton shook her head.

"That sounds nice." Daphne smiled.

"What? A ghost in our house? The hell it does!"

"No, silly," Daphne laughed. "Our house...I like the way that sounds."

"It is our house. I would've never made it to the point of building it, if it wasn't for you. Besides, many of the changes I made were with you in mind or came from ideas you gave me. It wouldn't be complete if you weren't there to share your life in it with me."

"I love you," Daphne whispered.

"I love you too."

"Oh, I almost forgot, we were invited to a costume party Friday night."

"Where?"

"Bridget and Wade's house."

"Oh really? Are we going?"

"I told her yes."

"My mother left me a voicemail this morning with the country club schedule. She's trying to push me to give her a date for the wedding."

"Yeah, my mom was asking too. I guess we'd better set a date soon."

"We haven't been engaged for seventy-two hours!"

"Calm down." Daphne smiled. "We can talk about it later. We need to figure out what we're wearing to this party. I was supposed to tell you about it Friday, but with the engagement and everything else, it slipped my mind."

"What do you want to go as?" Britton asked.

"I don't know, maybe you can find half of a horse and go as a horse's ass."

"Nice," Britton said.

"I, on the other hand, will be going as unemployed if I don't get back to work."

"Oh please, you're marrying the owner's daughter. I seriously doubt anyone is going to give you any shit."

"Still, I don't want favoritism either."

"Fine. Go back to work and slave away at your desk. How's that wet spot working for you, by the way?"

Daphne rolled her eyes and pulled Britton close for a slow, passionate kiss. "I love you and my wet spot and I hope I see you later," she said with a smile as she pushed her away.

Britton saw a few faces in the upper floor windows before the blinds swung back down. She laughed and slid into the driver's seat of her car.

Brides

Chapter 9

Britton got out of the passenger side of Daphne's car and closed the door. She'd been slightly surprised to get a call from Daphne not long after driving away from the distribution center, stating she'd decided to take the rest of the day off. When Daphne arrived at her townhouse, they'd decided to go shopping for their costumes.

"Do you want to be something cheesy like two sockets since we're technically not a plug and socket?" Britton asked.

Daphne laughed. "Are there going to be kids at this party?"

"I don't know. Do they know people with kids?"

Daphne shrugged as she texted Bridget. They walked around, looking at different tacky couples costumes until Bridget texted back.

"Looks like adults only," Daphne said.

"Sweet."

"You don't like kids, do you?"

"Sure, as long as they're not around me," Britton laughed.

"I guess we haven't really talked about kids. Maybe that's a conversation we should have," Daphne stated.

"Right here and now?" Britton raised an eyebrow.

"No." Daphne shook her head.

"Good. I'm not ready for another one of those fight things. That last one nearly wiped me out," Britton grinned.

"I don't know how to take that." Daphne pursed her lips. "And it wasn't really a fight to begin with."

"How about this one?" Britton asked, holding up a Wonder Woman costume.

"You'd look sexy as hell in that." Daphne grinned.

"Not me, for you."

"Me? No. But, I think you should get it though."

"I'm not wearing this to the party."

"Who said anything about the party?" Daphne bit her lower lip and wiggled her eyebrows as she walked to the other side of the aisle.

Britton wrinkled her face and put the costume back on the rack.

"Here's one," Britton said, walking up behind Daphne, who turned to see what she was holding.

"A pimp and his bitch?" She shook her head. "I don't think so."

"We're going to be here all night," Britton sighed.

"What about this?" Daphne asked, handing a pair of packages to her.

Britton looked at the gangster and pinup girl costumes and raised an eyebrow.

"How exactly, does this differ from the pimp and ho?"

"I'd rather be a gangster than a pimp and I think you'd be sexy as a pinup girl."

"I think you have our roles reversed. When is the last time you ever saw me dressed like this?"

Daphne laughed.

"Heather's wedding is the last time I wore a dress and my ass didn't hang out of it."

"Speaking of dresses…"

"If you say wedding I'm going to smack you over the head with this costume. Can we please figure out what we're wearing and get the hell out of here? We have plenty of time to talk about the big W."

"Well, what do you want to go as?"

"I don't know, but if I leave it up to you I might as well go in my underwear!"

Daphne laughed.

"Okay, this is the last aisle, so if we don't find anything here, we're going as a pair of sockets."

"Deal," Daphne said.

They walked up and down the aisle, looking at all of the pictures on the costume packages.

"This is perfect!"Daphne yelled from a few feet away.

Britton walked up to next to her. Daphne was holding a Wilma Flintstone costume in one hand and a Betty Rubble costume in the other.

"This is classic. Lesbians always joke that Wilma and Betty were hooking up while Fred and Barney were out doing stupid shit," Daphne exclaimed.

"Hmm? Really?" Britton looked over the costumes.

"They even come with the wigs and large jewelry!"

Britton couldn't help smiling and giving into Daphne's excitement.

"Okay, but I'm Betty. I refuse to be a redhead."

"Fine with me!" Daphne said, rushing to the register before Britton changed her mind.

~

Britton was sitting on Daphne's couch, using her chopsticks to dig through her Chinese takeout box while Daphne scrolled the TV channels for something to watch.

"That one!" Britton mumbled with a mouthful of food.

Daphne backed up to the Discovery Channel. They were showing a special about the most fascinating ruins of the world. She furled her brows and looked over at Britton.

"I love you and I love the nerdy side of you. I actually find it quite sexy when you curl up in front of the TV drawing, but I'm not watching this."

Britton frowned and bit into another bite of her food as Daphne continued scrolling until she found something they could mutually agree on.

"So, what are we going to do about this date dilemma?" Daphne asked, opening her own food box.

Britton wasn't ready for this conversation. Everyone wanted them to get engaged and now that they were, everyone wanted the wedding date. She was fine with getting engaged because the idea of a long engagement sounded nice. Sitting on Daphne's couch talking about the wedding date three days after getting engaged was not in her plans. She swallowed another large bite of food, seemingly so she didn't have to answer the pending question right away, and watched Daphne eat her Chow Mein. When Daphne's green eyes met her gray ones, she finally spoke.

"How about April…2016?" Britton bit the corner of her mouth.

Brides

Daphne laughed. "I seriously doubt your mother will fly with that date. I was thinking maybe March of next year."

Britton forgot to chew as she swallowed a large chunk of food, nearly choking on the wad of Lo Mein noodles. She set the box on the table and took a sip of her drink to wash down the rest of the remnants before clearing her throat.

"March? As in five months from now March? Doesn't that sound a little soon?"

"We got together in March, so it will be around our one year anniversary." Daphne shrugged.

"Oh. Do we really have to set an official date right now?"

"I know we just got engaged, but people are excited. Planning the wedding is the best part."

"It is?" Britton scrunched her face. "I thought the honeymoon was."

Daphne smiled.

"Maybe we should plan the honeymoon first. We might even need to practice for it." Britton wiggled her eyebrows.

"I think we've been practicing every weekend," Daphne laughed.

Britton leaned over, stealing a soft kiss before her phone began ringing. She looked down at the table and saw her mother's face on the caller ID.

"Way to go, Mom," she grimaced.

"You better answer it or she will keep calling. Your mother is nothing if not persistent."

Britton kissed her again, a little harder this time. "To be continued?" she grinned, raising an eyebrow.

Daphne rolled her eyes. "Answer the damn phone before I do it."

Britton pouted as she picked up the phone, sliding her finger across the face to answer it.

"It's about time you answered your phone. I was beginning to think you were ignoring me."

"No, I've just been really busy, Mother."

"I emailed you the country club dates. Did you take a look at them?"

"I haven't had a chance to." Britton looked at Daphne and rolled her eyes. "We were talking and March of next year sounds like a good month for us."

"Oh, March is no good. They're booked every weekend in March, April, and May already and part of June has already filled up."

"Wow...okay...what about July?" Britton shrugged, looking at Daphne.

"Your father and I were thinking December."

Britton titled her head to the side and Daphne nodded. "It's cold, but December of next year sounds good. A snow wedding would be really pretty."

"No, darling, December of this year," her mother corrected.

The phone slipped from Britton's hand, landing on the couch next to her. She heard her mother's voice as she fumbled to pick it back up.

"Hello? Britton?"

"I'm here. It must be a bad connection or something."

"Oh, okay. Did you hear me? The country club has December thirteenth and twentieth still open. I think the twentieth might be too close to Christmas though."

"That's a little too soon, Mother. Daphne and I just got engaged."

Brides

"Why waste time, darling? If you miss these dates, then you're looking at a late summer wedding and the country club is usually very busy that time of year. We may not be able to get the large reception room and the longer we wait, they may even book up into the fall."

"I see," Britton sighed.

"Talk to Daphne and let me know. I need to book it in the next day or two. I told her to go ahead and hold the thirteenth for me and I'd let her know by Wednesday."

"Yes, ma'am. I'll call you on Wednesday," Britton replied, ending the call. She slid the phone across the table and flopped back against the couch cushions.

"If it's any consolation, my mother called me this morning and mentioned a winter wedding," Daphne said.

"What did you say to her?"

"I told her we hadn't talked about it yet. Then, she tried to make plans to go dress shopping."

Britton shook her head. "What do you want?"

"I think a winter white wedding would be beautiful, but December is right around the corner."

Britton shrugged. "If there is anyone in this town who can pull off a wedding in less than seven weeks it's my mother."

"Trust me, mine's no slouch in the planning department either," Daphne added. "When she sets her mind on something, she goes balls to the wall."

"I love you, Daphne, and if this is what you want, then December thirteenth it is," Britton said, looking into the bright green eyes staring back at her.

"Did we just set our wedding date?" Daphne asked, setting her food box on the table in front of them.

Britton pursed her lips. "I think so."

Daphne smiled as she leaned over, kissing her softly. Britton deepened the kiss as she pushed Daphne onto her back without parting their lips. Daphne ran her hands under Britton's shirt, loosening her bra before pulling both up over her head. Britton sat back long enough to remove Daphne's shirt, then moved back down, kissing her passionately as their bare chests molded together.

They continued trading kisses as they wiggled around, trying to remove the clothing covering their lower extremities. Britton rolled to the side so Daphne could push her shorts down and lost her balance, falling to the floor with the squeak and a thud between the couch and coffee table.

Daphne peered down at her, trying to contain her laughter. Britton made a pouting face before laughing hysterically.

"Well," Daphne finally laughed. "That's a first. Are you okay?"

"What do you think?" Britton shook her head, still laughing. "It's actually quite cozy down here. You should join me."

"Um…yeah…no, I don't think so," Daphne replied, getting off the couch and offering Britton a hand up. "My bed is much more comfortable," she said, tugging Britton towards the loft stairs.

Britton wrapped her arms around Daphne, stopping her from climbing the stairs as she ran her hands over Daphne's bare torso from behind, mapping her territory as her hands slipped lower. Daphne leaned her head back against Britton, welcoming the contact and tangling her hand in the long hair at the back of Britton's neck. Daphne's shorts were removed when Britton tumbled to the floor, so she easily found the target she was lazily searching for.

Britton kissed the side of Daphne's neck while sliding her fingers through the wetness waiting for her. Daphne arched into her, before tipping forward and placing her hands on the wall near the staircase in front of her. Britton ran her lips and tongue over Daphne's shoulders, the back of her neck, then down her back, while one hand massaged her breasts back and forth and the fingers of the other rubbed languid circles over Daphne's clit.

Daphne moved in rhythm against her as Britton slowly played her body like a delicate instrument. Britton moved her mouth back up to Daphne's neck near her ear.

"I love the way you feel when I touch you," she whispered.

Daphne turned her head to the side, claiming Britton's lips in a searing kiss. Feeling her body begin to tighten, she turned away from the kiss. Britton pulled her fingers free, circling her clit one last time before dragging her wet hand down Daphne's thigh.

"Don't stop!" Daphne panted.

Britton spun Daphne around to face her and Daphne quickly wrapped her arms around Britton, pulling her close. Britton backed her up against the wall, kissing her hard as she pushed her fingers deep inside of her.

Daphne moaned against her mouth, pushing down on the fingers working in and out of her. She was too far gone to slow the cresting waves as the orgasm washed over her body. She jerked and writhed between Britton's warm body and the cold wall behind her. Britton kissed her softly and slowed her fingers, feeling Daphne tighten around them one last time, before slipping them free.

Then, she wrapped her arms around Daphne and held her as she caught her breath.

"My legs feel like rubber. I don't think I can climb the stairs," Daphne mumbled.

Britton laughed softly. "I don't think we both fit on your couch."

"It sounds like we have a dilemma," Daphne teased, looking into Britton's eyes, before pushing Britton back and climbing the stairs.

"I thought you couldn't make it?" Britton raised an eyebrow.

"I'd rather stumble on these stairs than fall off that couch."

"Nice," Britton laughed, following her up.

~

Britton was sitting on the bed when Daphne stepped out of the bathroom and walked over to her, pushing Britton onto her back. Daphne climbed on top of her, locked their hands together and leaned forward so Britton's hands were just above her head as she kissed her softly, pulling back when Britton tried to use her tongue to deepen the kiss.

Britton chased, stretching her neck, but failed to reach Daphne's mouth each time she teased her.

"Do you want this?" Britton said with a raised eyebrow.

Daphne smiled, biting her lower lip.

"You better stop playing with me," Britton threatened with a grin.

"Mmm or what? You going to spank me?" Daphne raised an eyebrow.

Brides

"Oh God, don't go all fifty shades on me, please," Britton grimaced.

Daphne laughed, leaning down to lick her nipples softly.

"You're enjoying this aren't you?" Britton writhed.

Daphne grinned and winked at her as she teased her lips once more. The loud ringing of the phone next to Daphne's bed broke their concentration.

"Is that your phone?" Britton asked.

"Yeah. It was in my pocket when I came up here to change clothes. I forgot to take it back down with me," Daphne replied, stretching for the phone on the nightstand. Looking at the caller ID and answered it while still sitting on Britton.

"Hey, my mom just told me she booked the country club for December."

"Nice timing, Bridge!" Britton yelled, hearing her sister's voice.

"What are you doing?" Bridget asked.

Daphne grinned. "Teasing your sister."

"Oh, gross."

Daphne laughed. "She likes to be paddled."

"The hell I do!" Britton shrieked.

"Wow, I could've gone to my grave not knowing that," Bridget said with a grimace. "Why did you answer the phone?"

"Maybe it was important," Daphne replied.

"Bullshit, don't let her lie to you, Bridge. She's a freak," Britton laughed, while trying to dump Daphne off of her.

"Okay, well it sounds like you two are having loads of fun over there. Daph, call me when you're not tangled around my sister," Bridget said as she hung up.

"Well, you just opened her eyes," Britton laughed.

"Nah, she was all into those fifty shades books when they first came out and tried to get me to read them."

"I'm beginning to think you did." Britton raised a questioning eyebrow.

"Oh, please." Daphne tossed her phone back on the nightstand. "Where were we?"

"My mother is already telling people and we haven't even given her the date yet."

"Can we not talk about your mother?" Daphne chided as she circled Britton's nipple with her tongue.

"Point taken," Britton moaned.

Chapter 10

The rest of the week had gone by in a blur for Britton. She'd started the sketches for the library, hired an assistant and a secretary, and had managed to pull the loose ends of her hectic schedule together long enough to witness the ground breaking for the new house. Daphne had been unable to make it because she'd had a last minute issue to deal with at the distribution center and she'd already planned to leave early for the party. Nevertheless, Britton had taken a few pictures with her phone to show her.

Britton was sitting at her dining table, flipping through the local history books she'd picked up from the book store on the way home when Daphne walked in.

"Did you know Rhode Island was the first to declare its independence?" Britton mumbled.

Daphne laughed, kissing her cheek. "What are you doing?"

"Research," Britton answered, sliding back from the table and pulling Daphne down into her lap. "I missed you today."

"I know. I'm sorry. I really wanted to be there. We had a freezer die on us and I had to route refrigerated trucks all over to get the meat out before it spoiled. But, before I could do that, I had to get the main office to okay a sale this weekend in the stores we service to make room for the incoming extra shipments."

Britton wrinkled her nose. "That sounds like so much fun."

"Organized chaos is what it is," Daphne replied, kicking her shoes off. "As long as I've worked for the company, I've never had anything this crazy happen. Maybe it's because today's Halloween, who knows." She looked down at the open book lying on the table. "What's this?"

Britton peered over her shoulder. "I met with the Cranston mayor this morning. He squeezed me a little on the library budget, but he liked the ideas I had. He wants something very historical, so I'm researching the state."

"I see." Daphne pursed her lips.

"I'd show you my latest sketches, but the last time I showed you sketches, they got all wet," Britton teased.

Daphne smacked her shoulder and laughed. "When do you want to go to your sister's?"

Britton looked at the watch on her wrist. "What time do we have to be there?"

"It's starts in half an hour."

"Can we be fashionably late?" Britton wiggled her eyebrows while sliding her hand up Daphne's thigh.

Daphne smiled, shaking her head as she pushed her hand away. "I promised we'd be on time. I was supposed to get off early to help decorate, but after the fiasco today, I told her I'd just come with you."

"Oh, you can definitely come with me. I'm sure she won't mind," Britton grinned.

Daphne rolled her eyes and kissed Britton softly before getting off of her lap. "Come on, we have to get ready. Your parents will be there. Do you really want to show up with the 'just fucked' look?"

"It's better than the sexually frustrated one."

"Please, you and I both know you're not sexually frustrated. You're like one of those dogs that walks around humping the air," Daphne said as she walked down the hallway towards Britton's bedroom.

Britton laughed. "You made me this way," she yelled after her as she stuck a sticky note in the book and closed it.

Daphne was in the middle of changing into her Wilma Flintstone costume when Britton walked in.

"Oh, that's a good look on you," she said, slinking up to her and stealing a kiss. "I've never been with a redhead."

"And you won't ever get to be either," Daphne chided, pushing her out of the way to look in the mirror and adjust the straps of her fake white dress.

Britton rolled her eyes. "I'm wearing shorts under mine."

"It is shorts, goofy. It's just made to look like a dress."

"Oh, thank God."

"Speaking of dresses, my mother wants to go dress shopping this weekend. I guess we need to decide our colors and to do that, we need to figure out our bridal parties, and to do that, we need to put a guest list together."

"Can we just go enjoy Halloween and do that another time? It's too much information to download in my brain at the moment."

"Another time? Britton, the wedding is six weeks from tomorrow."

Britton took a deep breath. She really wasn't ready to go over all of the wedding details. It really was too much for her to swallow at one time. She'd gone from dating, to getting engaged, to planning a quick wedding in such a short time that her head was spinning.

"Between your mother and mine, I'm ready to jump off a bridge. They're both calling me every day with this and that. My mom picked a florist, but needs me to go with her to choose the flowers. Yours wants to me to go with her to pick out a caterer and she emailed me videos of two different bands. Why aren't they calling you?" Daphne asked.

"They do. I just don't answer my phone." Britton shrugged. "My mom sent you videos? I didn't know she knew how to get on You Tube."

Daphne rolled her eyes and sighed. "Is this what you really want?"

"Of course it is. I love you and I want to spend the rest of my life with you." Britton wrapped her arms around Daphne.

"Then, do me a favor and participate, please."

Britton kissed her softly. "Okay," she whispered.

~

Britton grabbed a glass of something blood red and popped something gooey with a shell like a cake pop, that appeared to be an eyeball, into her mouth from one of the trays on the table. Bridget and Wade's house was decorated inside and out for the holiday. Their Tudor style home was the largest in the historic neighborhood they lived in, yet still vastly smaller than the estate she and Britton's parents lived in.

Brides

'There you are. I've been looking all over for you," Sharon Prescott said.

"I've been right here the whole time, Mom." Britton looked at her mother who was dressed as Martha Washington, and snickered. Her parents were nothing if they were not classy. She assumed her father was running around the party dressed as the first president.

"Daphne said she's going dress shopping this weekend with her mother."

"Yes, she mentioned it," Britton replied, eating another eyeball.

"Maybe you and I should go looking too. We all need to get together to figure out the bridesmaid dresses also."

"Bridesmaids?"

"Yes, darling. have you chosen a maid of honor yet?"

"Maid of honor? What? Mom, do we really have to do this right now?"

"Britton, the wedding in weeks away. This sort of stuff must be done as soon as possible," her mother scolded.

Britton sighed. "Alright. I'll call you tomorrow."

"You didn't tell me Heather was going to be here," Daphne said, walking up next to her.

"I forgot," Britton replied, pulling Daphne along before her mother could tie them down together in a wedding conversation. "What was that for? I've barely spoken to your mother tonight."

"She has W on the brain and it's not Washington. Where did you see Heather? She had to wait for Greg to get home, so they must've just arrived."

"I saw her near the bathroom...wait, here she is," Daphne exclaimed.

"Hey, aren't you two the cutest couple in here," Heather teased.

"Bite me," Britton growled. "Where's your better half?"

"I lost him at the open bar. Bridget really outdid herself this year. There are cars lined up and down both sides of the road."

"It's definitely her holiday. Any excuse to dress in a costume," Britton murmured. "I actually used to avoid these like the plague."

"Yes, I know," Heather replied.

"It's because you knew I'd be here, didn't you?" Daphne asked.

"Yeah," Britton sighed, biting her lower lip.

"It's okay. I avoided your family's Christmas party every year because I knew you'd be there."

"Aren't we all glad those days are over," Heather exclaimed, putting an arm around each of their shoulders and squeezing them close to her.

"Did you get into the punch?" Daphne laughed.

"No. Why? Is it hunch punch?"

"You're kidding me, right? This is Bridget's house. There's most definitely no hunch in her punch," Britton said.

"Don't look now, but here comes Bridget and your mother," Heather announced between the clinched teeth of her fake smile.

Britton kissed Daphne on the cheek. "I love you, but you're on your own. Good luck," she added, walking away with Heather.

~

Brides

There were less people out in the backyard since it was cold. A couple of propane heaters were lit in various areas and Britton walked over to the only one with no one standing near it.

"What was that all about?" Heather asked.

"This wedding shit is making me crazy. If it's not my mother hounding me about this and that, it's Daphne asking me. I'm ready to shave my head and request a padded room."

"Aww, it's not that bad. You knew what you were getting into when you proposed."

"Yeah, I thought a nice long engagement of a year or two or three. Not seven fucking weeks."

Heather nodded. "It is a little sudden. I was expecting a spring wedding."

"Nope, the country club is booked almost until next fall, but they happened to have December thirteenth conveniently opened to screw me over."

"If you feel that strongly about it, then why don't you say something? This should be yours and Daphne's decision, not both of your mother's."

Britton raised an eyebrow and crossed her arms. "I remember a few major issues you had to deal with because you didn't speak your mind, mainly allowing Leslie and your step-monster to be a part of everything."

Heather sneered. "If I could take that part back, I'd do it so fast your wig would fly off."

"Hey, I happen to like my wig," Britton said, adjusting the short black hairdo.

"Speaking of costumes and dresses—"

"I already know what you're going to say and the answer is I don't know. I am very uncomfortable wearing dresses. I did it for you and my sister because I would've

85

looked stupid up there in a pantsuit. I'm not really a tuxedo wearing kind of girl either. Daphne and her mom are going dress shopping this weekend and now my mother thinks we should do it too."

Heather laughed. "That ought to be interesting."

"I'm sure it will and you'll be there to witness it," Britton snapped.

"Why is that?"

"Because you're my best maid."

"Excuse me? Your what?"

"Well, my mother said I needed a maid of honor, but since I don't even know if I'm wearing a dress, I'm calling you my best maid. That way, all of my bases are covered."

"Nice," Heather laughed. "Wouldn't I be a matron of honor, then, since I'm married?"

"Best matron sounds stupid and you're not a groomsman. Oh, how about my best woman?" Britton smiled excitedly.

"I'm honored to be your best woman. You're my best friend and I love you to pieces, you know that right?"

"Yes, which is why you're going to help me through all of this before I have a damn stroke."

"So, since I'm your best woman, I'm assuming your party will be called the bride's men or is it the grooms maids."

"I haven't gotten that far yet, smartass."

Heather snickered.

"Can't it just be you? Do I really need a bunch of other people I couldn't give a shit about standing up there too?"

"Well, how many bridesmaids does Daphne have?"

Britton shrugged.

Brides

"Well, you should probably start there. Did you two at least pick out the colors yet?"

Britton shook her head.

"What are you waiting for? It's six weeks away!"

"Seriously?! Do you want me to smack you now or later? I just told you this shit is making me crazy and here you are giving me the same crap I'm getting from everyone else."

"Alright," Heather sighed. "You have to be somewhat involved, Britton. You asked Daphne to marry you and you're clearly head over heels in love with her. Just deal with this so-called shit for the next six weeks and it will all be over."

"Can we skip to the all being over part?" Britton huffed.

"As your best woman and your best friend, I'm going to give it to you straight, pun intended."

"I know."

"By the way, what's going on with the house?"

"They broke ground this morning. The foreman I have overseeing everything has worked with me on other projects and he's very thorough. With the crew they have now, we're looking at about five months. He told me this morning, if I hire an outside company to assist, we can possibly cut the timeframe in half."

"Wow, that's fast."

"It's costing me a fortune, but I'm meeting with another company on Monday to get the ball rolling and they have two large crews. I'd planned to be living in the house before the wedding, but I doubt that's going to happen."

"Cross your fingers. You got a huge three story office building completed in record time. If you have your way, you'll be moving into your new house before the wedding."

"That's true. Companies want to make money and they don't get the majority of it until the building is completed and passes inspection, so I guess we will see how money hungry these guys are," Britton said.

"Hey, speaking of hungry," Heather replied as her stomach growled loudly. "Do you think Daphne's gotten rid of your mother and sister yet? I'd like to go back in a find something to eat before I freeze to death out here."

Britton shook her head. "No one told you to come dressed as zombie whore."

Heather laughed. "I'm not a zombie whore, I'm Elvira."

"Well, she was a—"

"There you are," Daphne interrupted. "I've been looking all over for you."

"Good, you can have her," Heather said, heading into the house.

"Thanks for leaving me with your mother and sister. I love Bridget to death, but for some reason, planning her wedding seemed so much easier. Maybe it was because I was on the outside looking in. Now, I'm on the inside looking out."

Britton wrapped her arms around Daphne. "I asked Heather to be my best woman."

Daphne raised her eyebrows. "What's that?"

"You know, the person who helps me with everything and stands next to me at the ceremony."

Daphne laughed. "You mean a matron of honor?"

"No, a best woman. I'll explain later."

Daphne nodded and kissed her lips softly.

Brides

"Aww, aren't you two cute. I always thought Wilma and Betty were lesbian lovers."

"Go to hell, Wade," Britton laughed as Wade walked up in his gangster costume. He and Bridget were dressed as Bonnie and Clyde.

"Oh, here comes Daddy Warbucks. Nice talking to you," he said, scurrying off in another direction.

"I'm going to tell him you said that," Britton yelled after him.

"What's wrong?" Stephen Prescott asked, hugging his daughter and soon to be daughter-in-law.

"Nothing, Daddy. Just your son-in-law paying you a compliment."

"Oh." He nodded.

"I'm going inside, it's too cold out here for me," Daphne said, excusing herself from the business conversation she knew was about to start.

Chapter 11

The next morning, Britton awoke to the buzzing of an alarm. She knew she hadn't set hers since it was the weekend and she had no reason to be up at the crack of dawn. She pried one eye open and watched as Daphne turned the noise off and sauntered out of the bed towards the bathroom. She was naked and the slivers of new sunlight peeking through the blinds cast a soft glow on her silky smooth skin in all the right places.

When the bathroom door closed, Britton rolled onto her back and stared up at the ceiling. They'd fallen into bed exhausted the night before from the long week and staying out late at the party. Britton was still tired and could've easily slept another two hours, but she'd promised to call her mother and knowing Sharon Prescott, she was walking around with the phone in her hand.

Tossing the covers back, Britton crawled out of bed and meandered into the bathroom. Daphne was in the shower, humming along to the tune playing on the shower radio. Britton wondered if this was what it was like living together. She'd never lived with anyone but her parents and sister. She had tried living in the dorm in college, but after a couple of weeks she couldn't take it

Brides

anymore and had moved into an apartment near the campus.

The music stopped, followed by the running water, just before the curtain swung open. Daphne grabbed the nearby towel and began drying the water from her body.

"What are you doing up?" Daphne asked, noticing Britton at the sink brushing her teeth.

"The same thing you're doing."

"Dress shopping?" Daphne raised an eyebrow.

Britton watched her towel-dry her hair. "My mother wants to go shopping," she sighed.

"Are you getting a dress?"

"I'm not a dress person and I'm not a tux person. Maybe I should just go naked."

Daphne smiled. "I'd like that and I'm sure a lot of the guests would too, but I don't think the country club will allow it, babe." She finished drying off and stepped out of the shower. "What about a white pantsuit? No tie or anything like that, but pants, a jacket and a button down blouse. White heels or some kind of other white shoe would work with that outfit easily."

"Are you sure that's okay?"

"Of course. You're beautiful in anything you wear and I find you sexy in a pantsuit, especially with your hair falling in loose waves over your shoulders and the top few buttons of your shirt open, showing cleavage." Daphne leaned forward, kissing her.

"A pantsuit it is then," Britton replied against her lips.

"Is Heather going with you?" Daphne asked, stepping away to blow dry her hair.

"Yes."

"What's she going to wear?"

91

"I don't know."

"Well, you might want to figure that out before you go shopping."

Britton turned on the shower and stepped inside. A few seconds later, she popped her head out of the curtain.

"What are the colors?"

"Well, since it's a winter wedding and we're going with formal white for everything, I think the colors should be dark."

"How about blue, since it's your favorite color?" Britton asked.

"The color of your eyes is my favorite color, but blue is a close second, so yeah, I think dark blue would look nice."

"I'll get a list of blue and white flowers from the florist my mother is hiring and we can look at it this week," Daphne said.

Britton nodded and went back to her shower.

~

Britton pulled into Heather's driveway with a Pink song blaring on the radio. She got out with her head still bobbing to the beat as she pushed her sunglasses up on her head and walked to the door.

"You look excited about today." Heather raised an eyebrow.

"Not really," Britton replied as they walked out to her car.

"Did you at least figure out what you're wearing?" Heather asked, opening the passenger door.

"Yes."

Brides

"Good. I'm not prepared to listen to you and your mother argue all day. Where's she sitting by the way?"

Britton looked in the rearview mirror of her two-seater sports car and shrugged. "The trunk?"

Heather laughed as Britton put the car in reverse and backed out of the driveway, before putting it in gear and zooming off down the road.

"So, what did you decide on?"

"White pantsuit with matching shoes."

"What color white?"

"There's more than one?" Britton exclaimed, nearly blowing through a red light.

"Maybe I should drive. You're a little more high strung than usual."

"I am not high strung. I'm the most laidback person I know." Britton rolled her eyes. "Now, about this color thing—"

"It's simple. There's white, as in stark white, cream, oyster, champagne, ivory, bone, and ecru."

"Holy shit!"

Heather giggled. "The good news is, it's very easy to figure what color best suits a person. It's all based on their season."

"That's easy. The wedding is in the winter. What color goes with winter?"

"No." Heather shook her head. "Not the wedding season, your season."

"Huh?"

"Each person has colors that are associated with a season. You're supposed to go have your colors analyzed and that gives you an idea what palette is best for your colors. Each season is a different palette."

"What the hell are you talking about?" Britton laughed. "I don't remember you doing all of this color palette and season crap."

"That's because I did it with my mom. I knew there was no way you were going to sit through that."

"Well good, since you know these seasons, which one am I and which one is Daphne?"

"I don't remember all of them."

"Well, which one were you?"

"Autumn. I could've done summer, being that I'm more of a strawberry blond than a full redhead, but still, I went with autumn. You would be in a totally different season."

"Isn't this just wonderful. Since we're both wearing white, shouldn't Daphne and I be in the same shade? I wonder if she's doing this season thing?"

"I'm sure she is. I bet Bridget did it too. It's the first thing a reputable wedding dress shop does. Then, they show you the shades you can choose from. After that, they go over patterns and so on."

"Wasn't I there when you picked out your dress?"

"Yes, but I gave you a later time so that when you arrived, I'd be ready to try things on."

"Oh." Britton nodded.

"Since you're both in white, you can see if you have some of the same color choices in your seasons or simply chose to wear completely different shades of white."

"I don't even know where to look. Get on Google on your phone and figure this color thing out before we get to my mother's."

Heather began scrolling the internet as Britton drove them towards Newport.

"I'm glad you're coming with me."

Brides

"Why is that?"

"Because you'll need to catch my mother when I tell her I'm not wearing a dress," Britton said seriously.

Heather laughed, looking down at the buzzing phone in her hand. "Good news, Bridget said Daphne is going with regular white, so you should be fine in regular white too."

"Wonderful," Britton retorted, turning into her parent's circular driveway.

~

Sharon Prescott wasn't the least bit satisfied with the first two stores they went to and started making calls on her phone as Britton drove her mother's Cadillac CTS with Heather riding in the back seat.

"Head over to Wayland Square. Betty Toledo said she saw a new boutique with women's suits. Why you want to wear pants to your own wedding is beyond me," Sharon stated.

"Do we have to go over this again?"

"No, I've said my piece. What are your bridesmaids wearing, bowties?"

Britton rolled her eyes and Heather choked back a laugh.

"Right now, I only have a best woman."

"What on earth is that?"

"It's like a maid of honor and a best man."

Sharon spun around in the seat to look at Heather. "Are you wearing pants too?"

Heather shrugged.

"Oh for crying out loud, Mother. We haven't gotten that far." Britton turned into the plaza. "Do you know the name of this place?"

"No, she couldn't remember, but she said there were female mannequins in the window with pantsuits on."

"Oh great, let's ride real slow past each store until we find the lesbian mannequins," Britton laughed.

Heather held in her laughter as tears rolled down her face and Sharon simply huffed and turned to look out the window.

"There it is," Sharon exclaimed.

"Thank God," Britton muttered under her breath.

As soon as they walked into the store, Sharon went to work explaining what they were looking for and the occasion and Gerald, the gay man working in the store, went to work measuring Britton.

"Who's your wedding planner?" he asked with a slightly feminine voice and tiny lisp.

"We don't have one," Britton answered. "And why are you taking measurements, exactly?" she asked as he went up one side of her body, down the other, then around her chest over her boobs.

"I need to know what size suit you where," he answered.

"I'm a size six," she stated.

"I'm afraid our suits run in European sizes and instead of trying to convert everything, we simply measure you."

"I feel violated," Britton whispered to Heather, who hid her smile.

"Are you the blushing bride?" the man asked Heather.

She shook her head quickly. "I'm the best woman."

Brides

He scrunched his face as if he had no clue what she was talking about.

Britton rolled her eyes. "She's my straight best friend and she'll be standing beside me."

"Oh, okay. Well, you're going to need a suit too then." He stepped over to measure her.

"Wait, we haven't decided what she's wearing yet," Britton cut in.

"What about the rest of your party?" he asked.

"I have no idea. Right now it's she and I."

"I see."

"Let's just start with my daughter. Once we have her situated, we can work on everyone else," Sharon added.

"What color are we looking for? We have the traditional black, the modern gray, and the classic white."

"White. Also, I was thinking of no shirt. I like the look of the tight fitting vest under the jacket. Since it will be cold, I'm sure I'll be in the jacket all night, but if I take it off, I want the vest to fit as well as a low cut blouse," Britton said.

Gerald waved for her to follow him to the counter, where he proceeded to type a few things on the keyboard before spinning the monitor around for her to see the picture. It was a woman in a black suit with a matching five-button vest that fit her slender frame close enough to where there was no shirt underneath.

"Yes, that's what I'm looking for, but in white," Britton exclaimed.

"This is a very sexy look and most women are unable to pull it off," he paused, looking her up and down. "However, I think you can make it work."

"I think he just insulted me," Britton said as he disappeared to the back.

"He's probably jealous of your perfect boobs," Heather teased.

"They are far from perfect, but thankfully, they're not huge either."

"Want to trade?" Heather asked, looking at her smaller chest.

"So, you're going with no shirt or tie?" Sharon asked, changing the subject as she perused the small catalog on the counter.

"No. I'm definitely not a tie person and Daphne loves my cleavage, so I was thinking about how to make a tux look hot with being so stuffy and well, this idea popped into my head."

"It's a little risqué. What if one of the buttons pops off?"

"Mother, I'm sure my giant boobs aren't going to bust out," Britton replied sarcastically, looking at her modest sized chest.

"Is the vest going to be white too?" Sharon asked, ignoring Britton's comment.

"Yes, otherwise it will look like a prom outfit."

Heather snickered behind them.

"What do you want to wear?" Britton asked, turning around to face her.

"Whatever you want me to wear, I guess. I'm comfortable in anything."

"What are the colors?" Sharon interrupted.

"Blue."

"And?"

"Just blue."

Sharon raised an eyebrow.

Britton shrugged. "Dark blue to be exact."

"That's good because we were about to have to go over the fifty shades of blue," Sharon teased.

Britton's eyebrows shot up nearly to her hairline and Heather turned her head to hide her laughing.

"What?"

"Nothing, Mom. That's way more shades of blue than I ever want to know about," Britton answered, shaking her head. "Oh, look, here comes Geraldine."

"Britton Marie, he's going to hear you."

"Well, he's more flaming than a three dollar bill. I'm surprised he's not wearing a damn boa."

Heather stepped on her foot to shut her up as the man laid out the tux pieces on the table next to them.

"We have a fitting room over there," he pointed out. "Go ahead and try these on and see how they fit. We do our own alterations, so anything you need taken up or in, just let me know."

"Sure thing," Britton replied, trying not to mock his fake voice.

A few minutes later, she came out of the room wearing the vest and pants, and holding the jacket. Heather whistled, making her grin sheepishly.

"That's certainly going to get some attention," Sharon exclaimed. "You look beautiful, darling."

"Thank you," Britton replied, handing Gerald the jacket. "It's a little too tight in the shoulders. If I hug someone I may bust out of it like the Incredible Hulk."

"Oh, heavens," he said, scurrying away to find a different size.

"Are you sure you won't be cold? It is in December."

"No, I'll be fine. Are you sure you like it?"

"I think you look great," Heather added.

Gerald returned with another jacket and Britton slipped it on easily.

"Oh, this is much better," she said, buttoning the front.

"The good thing about this suit is, you can mix and match it. We find that most women like to mix and match their suits, so ours do not have the formal tuxedo satin lapel or stripe on the pants."

"That's even better." Britton smiled. "I'll take it," she exclaimed, heading back to the fitting room to put her jeans and sweater back on.

When she returned to the register, the transaction was already completed and Gerald was waiting for the clothes so that he could hang them in the zippered bag.

"I took care of it," Sharon stated.

"Mom, you didn't have to do that."

"I know I didn't, but I bought your sister's wedding dress, so it's only fair."

"What are you wearing for shoes?" Gerald asked.

Britton bit her lower lip in thought. "I don't know," she sighed. "Maybe heels."

"We have a sexy ankle boot style heel that just came in. It's available in gorgeous white silk, white patent leather and a few patterns like fish scales and snake skin with various colors, and it has a three inch, four and a half inch and six inch heel style."

"Let me see the three inch, white silk in a seven and a half and an eight, please," Britton said, following him over to the shoes.

Gerald went to the back again and came out with the two boxes.

"Those are perfect," Heather exclaimed.

Brides

"I have to agree," Sharon said. "This whole outfit is most definitely you. I think Daphne will love it."

Britton tried on both sizes to figure out which was best, then walked around the inside of the store to make sure they fit okay.

"I'll take these," she said, removing the shoes and handing the box to Gerald.

As soon as the transaction was finished, Britton left the store with her mother and Heather in tow.

"Well, that was easier than I expected."

"Yes, thanks to Betty. I'll have to send her a gift basket on Monday."

Britton wrinkled her face and looked at Heather, who simply shrugged.

Chapter 12

Britton was lying on her couch, flipping through the channels on the TV, when her phone rang. She smiled, seeing Daphne's face on the caller ID.

"Hey, babe. Are you just now getting home from shopping?"

"Yes. I'm exhausted. We went to five different stores and I must have tried on a handful at each place," Daphne sighed. "Most of them are long sleeves, which I do not want, and the ones that aren't just look tacky, with way too much lace or beads or don't come in bright white. I'm not getting married in ivory or ecru or any of those other off white colors. There are a couple of other places we're going to try tomorrow. Anyway, how did it go with you guys?"

"I bought something, and the shoes that match it too," Britton boasted.

"Seriously?"

"Yep. It's at my mother's."

"Is it a dress?"

"It's a secret."

"Britton, that's not nice. You know what I'm wearing."

"You'll see it soon enough."

Brides

"I'm not sure if I like the sound of that. Is it white or off white?"

Britton laughed. "It's definitely white. Heather started in on me first thing this morning and I had to learn all about seasons and colors and a bunch of other useless information."

"Yeah, me too. It's a good thing white works for everyone. So, what did Heather get?"

"Nothing yet."

"Is she wearing the same thing you are?"

"I don't know. Does she need to?"

"Well, you might need to figure that out soon. Bridget saw some beautiful dark blue bridesmaids' dresses. If she wants to wear a dress, they need to be in the same one."

"It's only those two right? You don't have a list of other people standing there with us, do you?" Britton asked.

"I was thinking about asking my cousin on my dad's side, since Heather is already in it."

"Can it just be us? You, me, Heather and Bridget?"

"What about the rings and flowers?"

Britton sighed. She was way over talking about wedding stuff. She wished she could just blink her eyes and go right into the next year. Bypass the wedding, bypass the holidays, and go directly to a fresh start.

"Did you hear me?" Daphne asked. "I guess we can have the flowers already on the aisle, or not even put them down at all. Bridget and Heather can hold our rings, which we need to go pick out by the way, in case they need to be sized."

"Okay." Britton closed her eyes. "Wait! You have a wedding band already. It goes to your ring. I have it in my jewelry box."

"That's good. I was wondering how I was going to match something to it. What about you?"

"Uh…I guess I'll look around and see what I find that's close to yours."

"Good. Let me know when that's done so I can cross it off the list."

"I was hoping to see you tonight," Britton said.

"I know, me too. Who would've thought wedding dress shopping would be so mundane. I don't remember Bridget having this much trouble, then again we drank a lot of champagne in the stores we were looking in. I didn't drink today since I was driving."

"You were offered champagne?"

"Yes, weren't you?"

"Nope."

"Aww, do you want me to pick you up your own bottle?" Daphne pouted.

"No, I'm over it."

"What are you doing for dinner?"

"I was hoping to see you," Britton answered honestly.

"Me too, but I'm tired and I have to get up tomorrow and do it all over again. Your father scheduled our inventory for this week since it usually takes place during the week that we'll be on our honeymoon. We are going on a honeymoon, right?"

"If we're doing anything, it's that. I promise you," Britton exclaimed.

"Good. Anyway, he changed the schedule last week, so now I'll be busting my ass all week and probably working twelve hour days to be ready for the scanning company to come in on Thursday."

"That sucks. I have to finish the preliminary library drawings and I also have a few other meetings this week too. Kathleen put two more bid sheets on my desk before she left Friday, but I left without looking at them."

"Who's Kathleen?"

"My new assistant. I told you about her."

"Um…no you didn't. You said you hired an assistant and a secretary. I assumed your assistant was male."

"No, they're both female."

"Maybe I need to stop in a see this Kathleen. Who's the new secretary?"

Britton laughed. "Kathleen is pretty, but she's married and over forty. She's worked in the building industry for almost twenty years and knows the municipality regulations and building codes better than I do. Now, Jenna, the front desk secretary, is a little younger than me with a cheerful, bubbly personality. She is just graduated with her associates degree and isn't sure she wants to continue school. I don't see her much, she's sort of Kathleen's bitch."

"Oh, nice," Daphne giggled.

"It's true. I talked to Michel, but he doesn't want to leave Phil Mason's firm, even though I offered him more money."

"You're better off without him anyway," Daphne said. "He's kind of an asshole if you ask me."

"Yeah, but he was a talented assistant. Anyway, Kathleen's doing a good job so far." Britton paused when she heard a doorbell. "Is that at your house or mine?"

"Well, unless you ordered take out too, that's my dinner," Daphne replied.

"No, I think I'll go to the gym and pick something up on the way home."

"Okay. I'll call you tomorrow," Daphne said. "I love you."

"Love you too," Britton replied before hanging up.

~

Monday morning had arrived quicker than expected. Britton was surprised to see how fast the weekend had gone by and not seeing Daphne for most of it, was a huge wakeup call. She showered and headed off to her office to see what was on the agenda for the day. Remembering the sketches on her dining table, she made an illegal u-turn and headed back to her apartment to retrieve them.

Finally arriving at the office, Britton flopped down in her desk chair, noticing the colorful sticky notes littering her desk. She began picking off each one and reading the message. Half of them were people following up on their interviews and the other half were actually work related. She quickly returned the mayor's call and set up a meeting for the middle of the week to go over the latest library building sketches.

The rest of Britton's morning was spent at the model table, next to her drawing desk, building the library model. She loved having the large office space with everything situated in one room. She no longer had to run back and forth between rooms when working on a project and if she needed to sit at her computer and research something, it was right there in the same room as everything else at her main desk.

Britton looked up from the desk when Kathleen walked into her office.

Brides

"The mayor's office just called. They needed to change the meeting from Wednesday to Thursday. I took a look at your schedule and went ahead and changed it. He's meeting you here in the conference room at two-thirty."

"That's even better, now I don't have to transport this model to his office. Thanks, Kathleen." Britton smiled and turned back to the table in front of her.

"Sure, I'm ordering in for lunch. Would you like something?"

"Anything, as long as it's not spicy or fried," Britton replied without turning back around.

~

Britton was the last one to leave the office on most days, and Monday was no different. She turned on her Bluetooth and listened to the half dozen voicemails on her cell phone as she drove home for the night. Three were from her mother with questions about the invitation designs and whether or not they found the matron of honor dresses yet. One was from Daphne about the flowers and one was from Daphne letting her know she emailed her pictures of the various blue and white flowers to choose from in case she didn't know what they looked like. The last message from was from Heather, wanting to get together one night for dinner. Britton called her back and left her a voicemail saying Wednesday night would work for her.

As soon as she arrived at her apartment, she changed into comfortable clothes and turned on the TV. Devouring the bag of Ying's takeout was her mission, but she stopped to check the email on her phone from

Daphne, first, and wound up scrolling through monotonous flower pictures as she ate her dinner.

Grabbing a pen, she made a couple notes on a napkin for the picture numbers she liked. When she was finished, she returned the email with the numbers she liked the best.

A few minutes later, her phone lit up with Daphne's smiling face on the caller ID.

"Are you sitting on your phone?" Britton answered.

"No, it's not as much fun as sitting on you," Daphne teased.

"Well, that can easily be arranged."

"I hate that we live so far apart," Daphne groaned.

"Me too. I don't know what to do on the weekends when I don't see you."

"When will the house be ready?" Daphne laughed.

"Not for another month probably."

Daphne sighed. "Anyway, you know I love you, right?"

"Yes…"

"We can't have five different blue flowers and three different white ones. We only need one of each."

"Then why did you send me a dozen of each?"

"I didn't. I sent you ten blue ones and six white ones."

"Oh for God's sake. I don't care what the flowers look like, Daphne. You decide. I gave you my choices, now you pick the two you want from those. It's that simple."

"I like the blue hydrangeas and the white roses together."

"What's a hydrangea?"

"It was number three. You liked it."

"Okay, then go with those."

"We need to know how many tables, how many bouquets, how many corsages, and how many boutonnieres."

"Okay, well we don't have the guest list done, so we have no idea how many tables. As far as everything else, you know how many."

"Do you want a bouquet?"

"No, a blue rose boutonniere for me, and white for our fathers."

"So you are wearing pants!" Daphne exclaimed.

"Damn!" Britton growled. The one secret she was trying keep flew out of her mouth like a cat out of a bag.

"I can't wait to see it! What about Heather?"

"Just put her in the same dress as Bridget and give them bouquets."

"What about the corsages for our moms?"

"What about them?" Britton asked.

"I was thinking white roses for them too."

"That's fine." Britton tossed the rest of her food containers in the trash and flopped down on the couch. "Daph, you know I know nothing about flowers, right?"

"Me either. These are all of the questions my mom bombarded me with today."

"Oh. Mine left a few voicemails too, something about invitations."

"Yes, she called me too, about the matron of honor dresses."

"For crying out loud, just pick a blue dress that comes in both of their sizes, how hard can that be?"

"Britton, it's a little more intricate than that. I told her Bridget's going shopping for them one night this week since I can't get down there until the weekend."

"Speaking of that, what are we doing this weekend?"

"I don't know what you're doing, but I'm going cake shopping with my mom and Bridget Saturday and Sunday we're working on the gift registry. Your mom mentioned something about checking out the caterer and going over the wine list. I believe she said you were doing that with her."

Britton blew out a frustrating breath. "She didn't mention that to me!"

"Well, talk to her instead of making her leave you voicemails!"

"Fine. Will I at least get to see you Friday night?"

"I'll be finishing this inventory and I have no idea how long it will take. I was here until midnight last quarter because those damn scanners doubled up on a section and it took me all night to straighten it out."

"Great," Britton said sarcastically.

"You sound tired. I'll let you go. Don't forget to look for your ring this week."

Britton said her goodbye and pushed the button to end the call. This wedding was looking less and less like organized chaos and more like a cluster fuck every day. The small, intimate wedding she and Daphne had originally talked about was long gone and had been replaced by something the Queen of England herself would be impressed with.

Chapter 13

Britton was sitting at the table in her office Wednesday afternoon, finishing the last touches of the triangular shaped model for the single story library building. It wasn't a very large building by any means, but the details behind the design were what made it stand out. The inside had a web of bookshelf sections on two sides, with the third side full of computer cubicles and microfiche film stations. A number of reading and work tables were near the middle where the triangular librarian desk was located. Each of the web sections had a different historical theme relating to the state.

"That looks neat," Sharon Prescott said from the doorway.

"It's the new Cranston library," Britton stated. "I didn't know you were coming by."

"I was in the area picking up the invitation samples, so I figured I'd bring them over to you."

Britton stood to hug her mother.

"I like the way you changed things around. That decorator you hired needed to go back to school," Sharon said, shaking her head.

Britton smiled. "You haven't met my new employees?"

"Of course. I just introduced myself."

"I see." Britton nodded her head.

"I'm proud of you, Britton. It takes a lot of skill to do what you do. Who would've thought that buying that Lego set you cried over in the store when you were eight would lead to this," she acknowledged, spreading her hands out.

"Thanks, Mom."

"Anyway, I didn't come here to get all sentimental on you. It must be these damn hormones."

Britton raised her eyebrows.

"Here are the invitations. I told her to give me all of the formal ones in white since it's a winter wedding and you're both wearing white. I also told her to give me a few samples of her dark blue ink colors and formal fonts. Take a look at these and let me know as soon as possible. We can't order them until we know the guest list though."

"Okay."

"I've already started the guest list for our side. Let me know of any friends or colleagues you want to add to it. I spoke to Daphne this morning and she and her mother have started their list too."

"Okay."

"I left you a message about going with me this weekend to meet with the caterer and also the country club bar to go over the wine and spirits lists and choose the champagne. We're going for Sunday brunch, so I will meet you there at ten. Bring Heather along. I invited Daphne, her mother and your sister, but they're doing the gift registry."

"Okay," Britton sighed.

"Did you put anything special on the registry?"

"A pistol," Britton answered nonchalantly.

"What?"

Britton smiled like a fake porcelain doll. "I was joking. I'll see you Sunday," she replied, ushering her mother out of her office.

~

Heather had a glass of wine waiting in front of Britton's seat when she arrived at the restaurant.

"You're a godsend," Britton declared, taking a long swallow as she sat down.

"It can't be that bad. The week's not over yet," Heather replied.

Britton tossed the folder full of invitation information on the table.

"What's that?" Heather asked.

"It'll be a miracle if I make it through this wedding," Britton huffed. "I'm supposed to pick the invitations out of that crap. My mother so kindly dropped it off at my office today."

Heather laughed.

"It's not funny. Do you see me laughing? I spent last night looking at pictures of flowers that Daphne emailed me, which most looked the same by the way, then, we talked on the phone so she could figure out which ones to go with and who needed what style and color."

"That's not so bad. What did you go with?"

"Blue and white."

"Blue and white what?"

"Flowers!" Britton exclaimed.

"Well, no shit. What kind of flowers?" Heather asked.

"I don't remember. Hydrants and roses, I think," Britton replied, perusing the menu and contemplating a much stronger drink.

"What the hell is a hydrant? Do you mean hydrangea?"

"Heather, you've known me over ten years. Have you ever seen me with a flower, talking about flowers, or so much as looking at them?"

"No," Heather laughed.

"I'm not as butch as it gets, but I'm also not Henrietta housewife either. I draw the line at some things, flowers being one of them. I'll go into the store and buy them for someone, but I don't care what they're called and the shades of colors they come in. I point to an arrangement or picture in a book and hand them my credit card."

Heather shook her head and laughed again.

"Oh, I forgot to tell you, we're going to Sunday brunch at the country to meet the caterer, pick the wine and some other shit."

"You'll like that. Let me know how it goes."

"I meant we as in you and me."

"Why do I have to be there?"

"Daphne, her mother, and Bridget are doing other stuff and I'm not doing this alone. My mother is making me lose my mind. Besides, she told me to bring you."

"What if I had plans?"

Britton raised an eyebrow.

"What time?" Heather asked, sipping her wine.

"Ten. I'll pick you up at nine-thirty," Britton answered as the waitress appeared.

Heather ordered and proceeded to open the large envelope, spreading the invitation samples all over the table.

Brides

"Oh my God, that's way too much to choose from!" Britton grimaced, ordering another glass of wine before the waitress left their area.

Heather separated everything out into piles. "It's not so bad," she said. "These are the backgrounds, these are the fonts, and these are the colors. You simply start with the background and pick one of each."

Britton picked up the background pile and spread them out in front of her. She mentally noted the differences in the lines and patterns. Choosing the one that looked the most modern and elegant, she slid it over to Heather and put the rest of them back in the envelope.

"See, that wasn't so bad. I liked that one the best too, by the way," Heather stated, sliding the fonts over to her. "I think these two are the most formal, if that's what you're going for."

Britton stared at both for a few seconds, then slid one over to Heather. As she placed the remaining fonts in the envelope, Britton looked at the colors.

"I didn't know there were this many damn shades of dark blue," she huffed.

"Me neither," Heather agreed. "You don't want royal or midnight blue because those are too dark and slate blue is too light. I like the azure and cobalt and the indigo is pretty too, but it does have a purple tint."

"I like the sapphire blue one," Britton replied, pulling that one to the side.

"Well, that's it. Now, you have your invitation. The stationary place usually makes matching thank you cards, so that will be easy."

Britton paper clipped the three pieces together and put the rest of the colors in the envelope.

"My mother is working on the guest list for my side. I bet it has five hundred people on it."

Heather snickered. "I'm going to be realistic and say three-fifty."

"I'll choke her," Britton muttered.

Chapter 14

Britton was waiting in the conference room when the mayor was shown in. The library model was sitting in the middle of the table with the scaled drawings laying next to it. Britton shook his clammy hand and proceeded to go over the outside of the model, then lifted the roof off to show him the various details of the inside. He pointed out a few areas in which she'd gone above and beyond his expectations, smiling often and touching her hand or arm to emphasis his points. Britton smiled cordially, trying to keep her distance. She opened the file folder next to the drawings.

"Go ahead and initial on the first two pages and sign the third one and I'll have all of the permits drawn up as soon as possible." Britton slid the pages over to him.

He pulled a pen from his pocket, initialing and signing where she had sticky note arrows.

"This project is already in the budget, so the permits should go through easily," he stated.

"Great. We'll be able to get started sooner rather than later." She smiled.

"Please join me for dinner tonight to celebrate and seal the deal," he said, stepping closer to her.

"I'm afraid I already have plans. I'm in the process of planning my upcoming wedding and I have appointments this evening."

He looked down at her bare left hand. "Maybe another time then."

"Perhaps after the completion of the build. My fiancé will be my wife by then and I'm sure she'd love to meet you and see the final result of this project." *Put that in your pipe and smoke it, you horny old toad.* She thought.

"Well, then." He cleared his throat and straightened his already perfectly placed tie as he backed up a step. "I look forward to seeing this project come to an end as well." He plastered a fake smile on his face.

"I will have my assistant email you copies of these documents today and as soon as I have the permit numbers, I'll have her send them to you as well."

He nodded and stepped out of the conference room. As soon as he was out of the building, Britton walked to the bathroom to scrub her hands.

~

Friday came and went without so much as hello. Britton was happy to welcome Saturday into her life. She was surprised to see how late she'd slept when she rolled over to look at the clock. Pounding on her front door grabbed her attention. She hadn't been expecting anyone and the thought of Daphne stopping by to surprise her made the butterflies in her stomach, take flight. She pulled a small pair of shorts and an old tank top over her naked body and rushed to the door.

"What are you doing here?" Britton snapped.

Brides

"Is that any way to greet your best friend?" Heather pursed her lips and pushed the door open to walk past her. "Get some clothes on. We're going shopping."

"Shopping? For what?"

Heather sighed. "I've been trying to call you for the last hour and a half, sleepyhead. My aunt called and asked if I'd go with you to Nordstrom to complete the gift registry there."

Britton scrunched her face. "What the hell do I need from Nordstrom?"

Heather shrugged. "Well, think of things for the new house. They have bedding, bath, home décor, kitchen, and dining accessories."

"I don't want wedding guests buying my bedding and bath stuff and I don't cook."

"Daphne cooks though, maybe think of things for her."

"The whole purpose for her doing the registry is because of that reason. She wanted some new kitchen gadgets and a china set."

"Come on, they have some neat vases, candle holders, and other tacky crap like that too," Heather teased.

Britton rolled her eyes. "Fine, but you're buying me Starbucks."

"Deal."

~

Heather walked around the store with the scanner gun, scanning various items to add to the registry while Britton texted back and forth with Daphne.

Do we really need all of this shit? **Britton texted.**

No, but if we don't register, the gifts will be worse, **Daphne answered.**

Wonderful, **Britton replied.** BTW, Heather is in charge of the scanner, so don't fault me when we get a bunch of tacky gifts.

LOL. I miss u.

I miss u too. I think I've forgotten what you look like, **Britton messaged.**

A minute later, Britton's next message was a selfie picture of Daphne with a huge smile on her face and her green eyes glowing in the flash. Britton's chest tightened.

Why r u wearing clothes? ☹ **Britton texted.**

LOL! The day I send u a naked pic, has to be the last day of my life so I don't give a shit who sees it.

Britton laughed.
"What's so funny?" Heather asked.
"Your cousin's sending me pictures."
"Naked ones?"

Brides

"No," Britton exclaimed. "That's what I was hoping for."

Heather said the pic should be nude.

OMG ur rubbing off on my cousin! LOL Got to go taste cakes. Love u! Have fun! Daphne texted.

"They're cake tasting. Why can't we be doing that right now instead of scanning toaster ovens?"
"I didn't scan a toaster oven. Do you need one?" Heather pursed her lips, turning to see where they were located.
"No! The point is, this is boring and I want the last hour of my life back!"
"Quit your bitching and come on. We're done," Heather scolded.
"Good, let's go get lunch. Some place that serves alcohol would be wonderful."
"Lush," Heather teased.
Britton raised an eyebrow. "You're lucky I love you, otherwise I might have just smacked you."
"Aren't you two cute." The lady at the registry counter smiled at them. "Oh, the big day's coming up soon," she said, plugging the scan gun into the computer to download the registry.
"We're not getting married," Britton retorted.
"What she means to say is, she and I aren't getting married. She's my best friend and she's marrying my cousin," Heather replied.

"Oh." The lady nodded, handing them a copy of the registry.

"Come on, honey." Heather linked arms with Britton. "Let's go feed and drown the beast that's starting to rear its ugly head."

~

Britton was sitting on the couch, answering her mother's mundane questions while flipping through the channels on the TV, when her phone rang with an incoming call.

"I have to go, Mom. I'll see you in the morning," Britton quickly toggled the calls to hang up with her mother and answer the other one. "Please tell me you're turning into my complex," she said.

"I just got home a little while ago. I'm sorry. I was exhausted when I dropped my mom and Bridget off and literally drove straight home," Daphne replied, kicking her shoes off and placing her feet on the coffee table.

"I can come out there."

"I love you, Britton, and I miss you terribly, but if you come out here, you both know we'll get no sleep and I have to be up early. Besides, aren't you meeting with the caterer tomorrow morning?"

"Yeah," Britton sighed. "We should've eloped."

Daphne laughed. "Why?"

"Because, we got engaged and all hell broke loose. I haven't seen you in two weeks and with the crazy schedules we both have, I may not see you until our damn wedding day." Britton sat up straighter. "Move in with me."

Brides

"We are moving in together, as soon as the house is ready."

"No, I mean now, before the house is finished."

"Britton, your apartment is small and we both have too much crap for that place. Plus, my job is an hour away from there with the traffic."

"Well, it's going to be even further when the house is built." Britton paused. "I really think moving in together would benefit us both. This wedding planning is crazy and our schedules are a mess, at least we'd be together every night."

"When you put it like that, it does sound like a good idea, but I have a lease, Britton. I can't just move out. I really don't want to have to pack everything up, just to unpack it and pack it again in two months."

Britton flopped back against the cushions in frustration.

"Are you there?" Daphne questioned.

"Yes," Britton sighed. "I think I'm going to go to the gym. I haven't been in a couple of days."

"Are you mad at me because I won't move in with you right now?"

"No, Daphne. I'm just frustrated with all of this. I've had a week from hell. The library model was accepted, despite my turning down the Cranston Mayor's advances."

"What?"

"That old bastard wanted to seal the deal, if you know what I mean."

"Gross. I hope you told him you've already sealed the deal with me and we're making it official in a few weeks."

"I did, trust me. I even told him I'd be bringing you to the ribbon cutting with me. He wasn't too thrilled."

"Oh well. Nasty old pervert," Daphne huffed. "My week wasn't much better. I worked until eleven last night finishing up the inventory. That's part of the reason I'm so tired. I've been working until eight or nine every night this week and haven't had much sleep."

"I've been coming home and working late every night too."

"Did you get the registry done at Nordstrom?"

"Yes. Heather did most of it."

"That's nice," Daphne laughed. "I can't wait to see what we get. It's probably a good thing she was with you."

"Yep."

"My mom and I finished the rest of the registry and ordered the cake. She wasn't sure of the guest list, so we went with the larger one that has four tiers. It's very wintery, white with frost colored snowflakes and a few other intricate designs. The top is actually two icicles melting into one and it's made out of sugar. It's beautiful. I think the people on the top of the cake are tacky and the wedding bells didn't really go with the design."

"It sounds pretty," Britton replied.

"I love you and I miss you. I should probably go to bed since I have a ton of things to do tomorrow. Have fun food and wine tasting with your mom."

"I love you and miss you too," Britton replied, before hanging up.

Chapter 15

The next morning, Britton picked up Heather and met her mother at the entrance to the country club. They were shown to a private room in the back and seated at a square table with the open side facing the kitchen.

"I don't think I've ever seen this part of the dining room," Sharon murmured, glancing around the room.

"What's on the menu?" Britton asked.

"I bet he knows," Heather answered, nodding towards the tall, thin man in a white chef's uniform, who was walking towards their table.

"Good morning, I'm the chef assigned to your event. I am to assume you are both the brides?"

"No," Heather laughed. "I'm the best woman. She's one of the brides," she said, pointing to Britton.

"Very well then. My name is Tony and I specialize in Tapas style cuisine. I'm assuming you're familiar with Tapas, since that's the catering style you chose, but I'll give you a little information about it. Tapas was originally a Spanish Cuisine, made up of appetizers or snack sized portions of various meals. It actually evolved into very sophisticated cuisine, taking the place of full meals, but served as entrees in a number of select bars. This concept carried over to Central America, and thus, became known worldwide."

Everyone at the table nodded. Britton and Daphne were fans of Tapas and so was Britton's mother, which was why that was the style of cuisine chosen.

Tony passed a strip of paper and a pencil to each of them. "We will be tasting appetizers, soups, main dishes, and desserts today. I will be sending a sample-sized portion of every dish to each of you. On the paper in front of you is the dish name and the numbers one through five. Once you tried the dish, circle the number that corresponds with how much you liked the dish. Five is the highest number and a perfect score and one is the lowest number. I will not be seeing these, so please don't worry about hurting my feelings. These are to help you finalize your decision. Also, the dishes will come in order and I'll explain each one as it comes out. You will need to choose two appetizers, two soups, three or four main dishes, two desserts, and one signature drink."

"This sounds easy," Britton stated. "Can we start with the drinks?"

"We like to finish with those," Tony laughed. "Also, there is mint and lemon water on the table for you to cleanse your pallet," he said, waving to the kitchen staff behind him. "We're going to go ahead and get started with the soups. These are served to your guests in shot glasses. We have a leek and lentil bean soup, butternut squash soup, broccoli cheese soup, pumpkin spice soup, and a seafood bisque."

The kitchen staff placed a small tray in front of each of them with shot glasses filled halfway with each of the soups. Britton worked her way from left to right, taking note that the leek and lentil bean was her least favorite. The broccoli cheese was okay, the butternut squash and pumpkin spice were pretty tasty, and the seafood bisque

Brides

was her favorite. She circled the numbers next to the soups and drank some of her water.

"Those were all very good." Sharon smiled.

Britton nodded in agreement and looked over at Heather, who pointed at the leek and lentil bean shot glass and scrunched her face. Britton grinned, making a face as well.

"Next, are the appetizers," he announced, as the kitchen staff returned with long, rectangle shaped plates that had the small portion of each of the dishes lined up. They put one plate in front of each person.

"Oh, these smell wonderful!" Sharon exclaimed.

"Here, we have ahi tuna on a lettuce bed, drizzled with a ginger soy sauce, classic escargot in a buttery herb sauce, crab cakes with remoulade, and baby artichokes stuffed with shrimp."

Each woman ate their bite-sized samples, one at a time, making sure to use the water between bites to cleanse their pallets. Britton enjoyed all of the appetizers, giving each one high marks.

"That crab cake was too dry for my taste," Sharon whispered.

"I don't care for artichokes," Heather added.

Chef Tony returned a few minutes later. "Now, for the main dishes."

Again, the kitchen staff returned with long rectangle plates, but these plates were twice as wide, leaving enough room for each of the seven dish samples to have their own section. Britton was glad she'd skipped breakfast.

"From left to right and top to bottom, we have filet mignon with roasted vegetables and sautéed spinach, almond crusted salmon with red wine sauce and wild mushrooms, grilled vegetable pizza with herbs and vinaigrette sauce, tuna tar tar wrapped in soy paper, pesto chicken with grilled vegetables, spinach ravioli with cream sauce, orange glazed roast duck with a red potato pancake."

Britton waited for him to walk away. "I don't even know where to begin. Some of these look too delicate to eat."

Heather laughed.

"Well, if it were up to you, we'd be serving some kind of take out," her mother scolded with a smile.

Britton shook her head in defense as she began trying the succulent bites. She liked the fact that each dish was completely different from the last, just as each of the appetizers were completely different from the main dishes. Heather wrote a few side notes on her paper as she circled her favorites.

A little while later, the chef returned to the table, followed by the kitchen staff who set square plates, similarly sectioned off the way the main dishes had been, in front of each of them.

"Finally, the desserts." He smiled. "We have white chocolate and raspberry mousse in a chocolate cup and with a chocolate spoon, all of which are edible, scoop of vanilla lavender ice cream, finished with white chocolate décor, classic bridal cake pop with a red velvet center, vegan chocolate cake with warm chocolate sauce drizzled over it, and lemon bars crusted with graham cracker."

"I don't know about the two of you, but I'm stuffed," Sharon said, staring at her dessert plate.

"Me too, but these look divine!" Britton exclaimed, starting with the mousse first. "Oh my God, that's good!"

Brides

Heather started with the ice cream and Sharon went for the lemon bar.

As soon as everyone had finished with their dessert plates, the kitchen staff cleared the table and the chef came back out to see them.

"Tony, everything was exquisite. Thank you so much," Sharon stated. "It may take us a few minutes to sort through our notes and make our final decision."

"Mrs. Prescott, please take your time. The bar staff will be bringing over the signature cocktails in just a moment. They are shot glass sized for sampling. The first is called the Frozen Moon. It's vanilla vodka on the rocks and the rocks are actually frozen blue Curacao made to look like ice cubes and it's served in a rocks style glass. The second drink is called Spanish Peach. This one is peach schnapps and tequila with a splash of vanilla vodka and served on ice in a highball glass. The last one is called Holiday Cheer. It's apple vodka, vanilla vodka, peppermint schnapps, a splash of dark rum and a splash of cranberry juice, served on ice in a Collins glass or highball glass."

"Those sound good." Britton grinned.

"I have to agree with you on that one," Heather added.

"Traditional wine and champagne will be served as well. I believe the bar will be going over this lists and sampling those with you shortly," he said. "If you have any menu questions, please feel free to ask and again, thank you for choosing us to cater your event."

They gave Tony a small round of applause before he left the room.

"Okay, ladies, let's get down to business before the booze arrives." Sharon smiled. "What did you think of the appetizers?"

"Personally, I'm surprised there was no vegetarian appetizer to choose from. They were all seafood related," Heather said.

"I noticed that too," Sharon replied. "Also, there wasn't a salad dish either."

"The ahi tuna dish and escargot were my favorites," Britton declared.

"Okay." Sharon circled those two on the main paper for the chef. "What about the soups?"

"Leeks and lentil beans are gross and to put them in a soup is a waste of time," Britton stated.

"Yeah, I definitely agree with you," Heather added.

"Which two were your favorite?" Sharon asked.

"Seafood bisque and pumpkin spice," Britton answered.

"See, I liked the butternut squash," Heather stated. "The pumpkin wasn't bad though."

"What do you think, Mom?"

"If the appetizer has seafood and most of the main courses, then I think we should go with the pumpkin and butternut squash soups."

"That's probably a good idea," Heather agreed.

Britton pouted. "That damn seafood bisque was excellent though."

"It was good. I'm not denying that, but we have to be practical," her mother chided.

"Alright, what main dishes did you like?" Britton questioned.

"We need three or four of those and to be fair, let's go with four, so that we cover the food groups.

Brides

Personally, I think the tuna tar tar should have been an appetizer. Other than that, we need a meat dish, a poultry dish, a seafood dish, and a vegetarian dish. So, the filet mignon, the almond crusted salmon are obvious, and I think the pasta dish and the chicken dish work well together too."

"I liked the duck, but the chicken pesto would probably be more popular," Heather added.

"Well then, I think we have our list," Britton exclaimed. "Perfect timing too, here come the drinks."

A tall brunette stepped up to the table with an ear to ear smile on her face. Her hair was wrapped in a loose bun at the base of her neck and she was wearing a skirt suit with a little too much cleavage showing at the front of her blouse.

"Hello ladies, I'm Maria and I'll be walking you through the wine and champagne tasting, but first, we have the signature cocktails for you to sample. I believe Chef Tony went over them with you," she said, passing the shot glasses out and allowing her eyes to linger a little longer than necessary on Britton.

Heather cocked her head to the side and raised an eyebrow as the woman handed her drinks to her. The woman turned her head quickly and stepped away from the table to grab her wine and champagne lists. The chilled bottles were already sitting in ice buckets at an adjacent table.

"I like the Frozen Moon the best," Britton stated. "I looks cool and it fits our blue and white theme."

"I'm not a big liquor drinker, so the choice is yours," Sharon replied.

"The tequila is too overpowering in the second glass and the third tastes like a stick of peppermint laced with applesauce. Definitely go with the first one, Britt." Heather quickly drank some water to wash the taste of the drinks from her mouth.

Sharon circled her choice and took it up to the dining room manager. When she returned to the table, Maria was passing out the wine and champagne lists and explaining the process.

"She could tuck those things in a little tighter," Heather chided when Maria walked away.

Britton laughed. "She's just looking for attention."

"Yeah, yours. She keeps staring at you."

"No she's not," Britton replied, shaking her head. "Maybe she's into you, or she has the hots for my mom."

"That'll be the day," Sharon retorted, causing everyone to laugh.

"It looks like everyone's in the mood for wine tasting." Maria smiled as she returned to the table. "I took a look at your menu choices and put together our best pairings for you to choose from. I have some chardonnays and sauvignon blancs that will go well with the seafood and poultry, as well as a couple of merlots that will pair with anything," she said as she began pouring a sample of each wine for them to taste.

Britton swished the liquid around in her glass, smelling the aroma before taking a sip. Her mother and Heather followed suit until they'd tasted wine from each of the bottles on the table.

"I think the Cakebread or Ferrari Carano Chardonnays are the best," Britton declared. "I actually buy these both from time to time.

"That's my favorite as well," Heather replied. "I can't decide between the Sterling or the Stag's Leap for the merlot. I like them both."

Brides

"I've never had the Sterling merlot, but this is pretty good." Sharon nodded, having an extra taste. "My favorite red is Conundrum and my favorite white is Far Niente."

"Oh, yes, Far Niente is my favorite too. Is that one not available?" Britton asked.

"Yes, ma'am, but at seventy dollars a bottle retail and nearly sixty-five a bottle per case, we don't usually stock it for large events. If you'd like, we can special order it though."

"I don't think we need to special order anything. The Cakebread chardonnay and the Sterling merlot are both excellent wines. Let's go with those," Sharon said to Maria.

"Excellent choices," Maria replied, making notes. "Now, for the champagnes. I put together the most popular two bottles of each classification, dry, extra dry, and brut. This also includes a few sparkling wines which are somewhat more popular than traditional champagne."

Britton started taking small sips of each of the samples, but couldn't tell one from the other, except for the variations of dryness. She wasn't a big fan of champagne, so she relied on her mother's expertise with this choice.

"Which one do you like, mom?"

Sharon tried a few samples and continued searching for the best flavor. "I'm not sure. What about you?" she answered.

"I don't think I like any of them. Heather?"

Heather shrugged. "I'm not really a fan of champagne."

"I think either the Mumm Brut Rose or the Chandon Reserve Cuvee."

"I believe we served Chandon at my wedding and it was pretty good, but I'm not sure which one it was and I'd also had a lot of it." Heather smiled.

"I remember it wasn't bad," Britton agreed. "Go with the Chandon Reserve Cuvee, Mom."

"Another excellent choice," Maria said. Turning to Sharon, she asked, "How many guests will be attending?"

Sharon looked at her daughter and sighed. "We're still working on the guest list, but I should have that information to you this week. The reception room holds three hundred, so go ahead and estimate it at that for now."

"Three hundred!" Britton exclaimed. "Mother, that's way too many people. I don't even know three hundred people, at least not close enough to invite them to my wedding!"

Heather looked at her best friend and shrugged.

"Darling, we'll talk about the guest list later," Sharon murmured.

Britton thanked Maria for her service and walked outside. Heather found her leaning against the side of her car with her arms crossed over her chest and her dark sunglasses covering her eyes. The breeze blowing Britton's hair around her shoulders was cool, indicating the upcoming winter weather change was around the corner.

"She's off her rocker if she thinks we will have three hundred guests," Britton spat. "Did Bridget have that many?"

"I don't remember, but it was a lot," Heather replied. "Look at it this way, it's only one day and then it will all be over."

Brides

"One perfect day has turned into a whole hell of a lot of miserable ones," Britton sighed. "What a buzz kill."

Heather laughed. "I think I ate too much to get a buzz off the small sips I took."

"True. That food was excellent."

"Hello, ladies," Sharon said, walking up to them. "Britton, I know that sounds like a lot of people, but we have family, close friends, and business associates that want to share this special day with us and with you. Does Daphne and her family have their list ready yet?"

"That doesn't include her list?" Britton shrieked.

"Well, of course it does. If the reception room holds three hundred, then both families are entitled to one hundred and fifty guests each."

Britton's jaw nearly hit the floor. Her small, intimate wedding was turning into a stage production with an enormous audience.

Sensing her best friend was about to have a meltdown, Heather quickly stepped up next to her.

"I hate to cut this short, but remember I promised Greg I'd be back in time to help him with that project," Heather interjected.

Britton raised an eyebrow.

Heather made a stern face and nodded towards the car.

"Oh, yeah, I forgot. Mom, I need to get Heather home since she rode with me. I'll call you tomorrow." Britton quickly hugged her mother and got into her car before she was conned into doing some other wedding type activity.

"Thank you," Britton said to Heather as she drove them out of the parking lot.

"I thought you were going to smack her," Heather laughed.

Britton shook her head. "I should have. She's seriously lost her damn mind, that's for sure. Wait until Daphne hears about this."

"How's she doing with everything?"

"Fine, I guess. I haven't seen her since Halloween. We've both been too busy with work during the week and this wedding crap has been taking up our weekends."

"That explains a lot. No wonder you're on edge. You two are usually so wrapped up in the sheets every weekend that you barely come up for air."

Britton smiled and shook her head as she downshifted to come to a stop at the red light. "I have a healthy sex life. You should try it," she teased.

"Countless hours of sex all weekend long? No, thank you. I like to spread it out throughout the week. Besides, I don't think Greg could go that many times back to back."

"Oh, gross. I didn't need that visual."

Heather giggled. "Anyway, back to the guest list, I can't imagine my aunt inviting a hundred and fifty people. I don't even think she knows that many people. You saw how big my family was at my wedding, so figure about that much for her side, plus friends."

"It's still too much," Britton grimaced. "My mother is apparently inviting all of Rhode Island!"

Heather laughed and Britton raised an eyebrow, giving her a dirty look.

"It's not funny. Shall I invite your step-monster and her spawn? I'm sure they'd love to sit with you."

"Well, for one, I'll be standing next to you at the ceremony and I'll be sitting next to you at the reception since I'm in the wedding party. So, really, they'd be

Brides

sitting with my mother and step dad. So, if you want a wild west showdown, by all means, invite them."

"That might not be a bad idea. At least we'd have some entertainment," Britton laughed.

Chapter 16

Monday morning was chaotic in Britton's office. She spent the first part of the day on the phone returning voicemails and on the computer replying to emails. Lunch had come and gone without notice when her cell phone buzzed on the desk with a new message.

Did u go over the song list from the band? Daphne texted.

Hello to u 2 and no, I've been busy all day, Britton replied.

I need to get the band booked unless u want a DJ.

Britton blew out a frustrating breath. *I don't give a shit if we play mixed tapes, at this point. I'm over the whole thing.* She thought as she filled out the PDF permit forms on the computer for the library.

Do whatever u want, Britton texted.

What's that supposed to mean?

Brides

It means I'm working and music isn't really on my mind at the moment.

Fine! Did u at least call the photographer? Daphne texted.

"Damnit!" Britton growled, making a mistake on the form. Now, she'd have to start all over.

I'm really busy with the library permits. Can u call her?

I'm working 2! This stuff has to be done!

Britton contemplated tossing her phone against the wall. She ignored the latest text and started the PDF form over. A half hour later, her cell phone rang. She couldn't ignore the smiling face looking back at her from the caller ID.
"Hey," Britton answered.
"Are you ignoring me?" Daphne asked.
"No," Britton sighed. "I'm really busy and this wedding stuff is the last thing on my mind."
"I'm working too, but we are running out of time. I promised my mother I'd have the song list to her by tomorrow and she's trying to put the deposit down on the photographer, but she wasn't sure how much it was since everyone we talked to was a different rate."
"I'll send you the song list tonight and call her as soon as I get the forms finished. I have to get them

139

emailed to the judge today. He's going to expedite them for me."

"I thought you had issues with him?"

"I think he got the hint that I wasn't going to screw him to get the deal, so he moved on and is ready to get this project over with. Personally, I don't think he's used to be told no, but even if I was straight...gross, I can't even think about that scenario."

Daphne laughed. "That's good to know. By the way, did you get your ring yet?"

"No. I'll do it this week."

"I emailed you the server settings and flutes. We need to get those picked out so my mother can get them ordered, so email me back the ones you like."

"Okay. Hold on," Britton said when Kathleen walked into her office.

"I just got off the phone with Jay Dewitt, the guy with the bar on the water. He has some questions about the bid. I set up a meeting with him tomorrow morning."

"That's great. Thanks, Kathleen." Britton put her cell phone back to her ear and heard the dial tone. "Isn't that nice," she growled, turning her phone off and putting it in the side pocket of her briefcase.

~

By Tuesday night, Britton had finally sent the music list, left a message for the photographer and emailed Daphne the flute and server choices, which she thought was stupid since they'd all looked the same to her.

She had spent most of Wednesday rewriting the bid for the bar after the owner explained the changes he wanted and the budgetary constraints he'd been given by

Brides

his business partners and had finally left the office around seven that night.

Britton had just poured herself a glass of wine and sat down on her couch when her cell phone rang.

"Congratulations," Heather said when Britton answered.

"For what?"

"I saw your announcement in the paper today."

"Announcement?" Britton questioned, sipping her wine. "For what?"

"The wedding," Heather replied.

"Oh, that must've been my mother's doing. I didn't know you needed to announce those things, but then again, she's inviting the state so maybe it's just one big invitation. What did it say?"

"Here, I'll read it to you." Heather paused for a minute and came back on the line. "Mr. and Mrs. Stephen Prescott are pleased to announce the engagement of their youngest daughter, Britton Prescott, to her partner, Daphne Atwood. The upcoming wedding will take place on December 13, 2014."

"Wow. Way to announce it to the world, mom," Britton said dryly.

"I think it's nice."

"I don't remember you having your wedding plastered all over the paper."

"I didn't, but you're a Prescott. Everyone in this state shops at your family's stores. Besides, it's not plastered. It's a small picture of the two of you with the words under it."

"A picture! Are you serious?!" Britton squeaked.

Heather laughed. "It's not very big and it's black and white. It looks like it was taken at your parent's house near the cliff overlooking the coast."

Britton swallowed the last of her wine in one large sip and poured another glass. "I know which picture you're talking about. It was taken on Father's Day and as a matter of fact, Bridget took it."

"It's a nice picture of the two of you."

"Yes, nice for us to enjoy, not the entire world," Britton huffed.

"Oh, quit pouting. Did you get the band and photographer hired?"

"Yes and if one more person asks me that I'm going to chuck my phone against the wall. Can I just enjoy a peaceful evening without being hounded by wedding crap? Oh wait, you blew that for me."

"I know wedding planning isn't easy. It's actually a fact that wedding planning makes a couple much stronger. Those who can't make it through the planning, never make it down the aisle."

"Yeah, well, I may not make it to the end of this week, much less down the damn aisle."

Heather laughed at her best friend, but she knew the frustration was starting to wear her thin. "I'll let you go so you can relax. Call me this weekend if you want to get together. Greg's going hunting with a guy from work. I'm not sure I like that idea and it's not something he's shown interest in before now, but I don't question some of the odd things he picks up from time to time. As long as he doesn't come home with some dead animal and try skinning it in my front yard, we're good."

Brides

"Gross," Britton grimaced as she yawned. As soon as she set the phone down it rang again. "Oh for God's sake," she snapped, answering it again.

"Is everything okay?" Daphne asked.

"Peachy. How are things with you?"

"I'm tired. My mother said there's an engagement and marriage announcement in the paper there today with our picture in it."

"Yes, I was informed as well. I'm sure that's at the hands of my mother."

"I see," Daphne said. "Did you get your ring?"

"I'm going tomorrow after work. I was busy rewriting the bid for that bar I told you about. The owner's business partners are tightwads, so he had me basically redo the entire thing."

"That sucks. What about the marriage certificate? That has to be applied for in your county since I live out of state."

"I know. It's on my list."

"Speaking of lists, my mother and I worked on the guest list Sunday and again last night over the phone. It should be done in a day or two and I'll email it to your mom this weekend."

"Don't even start that conversation," Britton huffed.

"What do you mean?"

"It's a long story, but my mother is inviting the whole state."

"What do you mean the whole state?"

"The reception room fits three hundred people, so she told them to go ahead and expect that many."

"I guess that makes sense," Daphne replied.

"Makes sense how?"

"Well, with your family, my family, then all of their friends and our friends, I can see over two hundred easily."

"Two hundred guests…at our wedding?" Britton shook her head.

"How many are on your list?"

"I don't know. My mother's working on it and I'm supposed to add in anyone she leaves out."

"Britton, you're family knows a lot of people and I'm an only child, so my entire family will be there and my parent's close friends."

"I still think two or three hundred people is ridiculous."

"We aren't exactly having a small wedding and now that your mother has announced it to the state, I'm sure people will be coming out of the wood work, fishing for an invitation."

"Well, tell them no," Britton growled.

"Are we seriously arguing about the guest list number when we don't even know what it is?" Daphne asked.

"I don't know. I guess we are."

"Bridget had a large guest list too."

"I was too distracted at her wedding to pay attention to what was going on around me," Britton murmured.

"Yeah, me too. Some maid of honor I was," Daphne laughed.

"We're lucky my parent's didn't throw us both off the cliff."

"Your parents? I thought for sure Bridget would never speak to me again," Daphne exclaimed. "It seems like it was yesterday."

Brides

"It was! Did you think we'd be getting married nine months later, almost to the date?"

"Well, no, but here we are. It's too late to back out now."

"Is it?" Britton sighed.

"Are you having second thoughts?" Daphne asked seriously.

"No. I'm just tired."

"You scared me for a second there. Besides, I tried my dress on yesterday for the first fitting and you're going to love it. I go back in two weeks to finalize everything."

Britton shook her head and smiled. "I miss you," she said.

"I miss you too."

"What are you doing this weekend?"

"I have a late meeting Friday, but my weekend is free."

"Not anymore. You're spending it with me."

"That sounds like a wonderful idea," Daphne replied.

Chapter 17

Britton was sitting at her desk Friday afternoon, contemplating taking off early because she'd have enough for one week, when her phone vibrated. She looked down at the message with a raised eyebrow.

Congrats...I think LOL. Saw the announcement. Let's grab a drink, Victoria texted.

Britton stared at the message. A drink sounded good, but she wasn't sure if seeing her ex-girlfriend, Victoria was the best idea. Never the less, she threw caution to the wind and texted her back.

Sure. I have some errands to run downtown. C'est la Vie at 6?

See u then, Victoria texted back with a smiley face.

Britton turned off her computer, wrapping up her day, as well as her week. She checked with both of her employees to make sure she didn't have anything else pending for the week and told them to have a good weekend, before walking out the door. She pulled her suit jacket closed, buttoning the two buttons to stave off the cold air as she walked to her car.

~

After a stop at the jeweler, Britton arrived at the restaurant. She locked her briefcase in the trunk and walked inside, spotting Victoria sitting at a small table in the bar area in a low-cut, black dress with a long slit up the side and black, pointed-toe stilettos.

"Aren't you cold?" Britton asked, sliding into the seat across from her and unbuttoning her jacket.

Victoria grinned. "Are you offering to warm me up?"

Britton laughed. "Don't hold your breath."

"A girl can dream can't she? Lord knows I have enough memories to get me through the cold nights rather warmly."

Britton shook her head, ordering a glass of chardonnay from the waiter.

"Did you invite me here to try and sleep with me? If so, it's not happening."

"No. I'm actually surprised by the ad in the paper and I wanted to see for myself if it was true," Victoria stated.

"It's not an ad and yes, it's true. Daphne and I are getting married."

"I thought you never wanted to get married. In fact, you used to make fun of weddings, calling them a dog and pony show."

"People change."

"It's a little sudden isn't it? Is she pregnant?"

"Pregnant? You dated me for how many years? Did you ever see a penis attached to me?" Britton exclaimed.

"Well," Victoria paused, grinning succulently. "There was that one time…and oh, what a time that was," she replied, licking her red lips.

Britton's cheeks colored slightly. "Yes, well, that was a long time ago and no, Daphne's not pregnant or intending to get pregnant. We're in love and we're happy. Marriage is the next step."

Victoria shrugged. "If you say so."

The waiter deposited Britton's drink and walked away. She took a long sip.

"I don't mean anything against the time you and I shared together, but Daphne and I have a history that bonded us together a long time ago. It just took a long time for us to figure it out. I love her."

"I know, it's sickeningly sweet how into each other you are," Victoria said, rolling her eyes.

Britton raised an eyebrow.

"I saw you together a couple of months ago at WaterFire."

"You did?" Britton asked, sipping from her glass. "Why didn't you say something?"

"I was a little shocked to see you all over each other, but I always knew you'd get together eventually." Victoria shrugged.

"What made you think that?"

"Because you hated each other so damn much. Those we hate the most are the ones we can't live without."

"Hmm. I guess that makes sense in a creepy sort of way. You still could've said hi."

"I was on a date."

"I see…and?"

Brides

"And what?" Victoria sipped the last of her wine and checked her phone before ordering another glass. "We screwed and moved on," she replied nonchalantly.

Britton smiled and shook her head. "How did you and I stay together for so long?" she sighed.

"If you recall, it was on and off and the sex was hot. We kept coming back for more," Victoria replied.

Britton nodded in agreement.

"I can't fault her though…you're soon to be wife, that is. Anyone who can tie you down, must be a goddess in bed."

Britton laughed. "It's a lot more than that. She's a hell of a woman."

"Still, Britton Prescott…getting married? Maybe I need to play the lottery, either that or prepare for hell to freeze over."

Britton shook her head. "I forgot how well you know me," she laughed.

"Putting a ring on your hand is one thing, but getting rid of that bad girl who's buried deep inside of you is a whole different story."

"I let her go the moment I realized I was in love with Daphne. My playing days are over."

"I'm sure your parents had a lot to do with it. I knew eventually they would push you to get married and see things their way. I'm surprised you're not running the company now that you're settling down."

"Actually, I have my own design firm now."

"Wow. That's great. What does daddy think?"

"My father is actually a silent business partner."

"Hell is definitely freezing over if your dad has stopped trying to make you take his place and is accepting your career choice."

"Yeah. I guess a lot has changed this year," Britton said.

"I'd say so." Victoria sipped her wine. "Is this really what you want?"

"You mean getting married? It's the next step in life. I want to spend the rest of my life with Daphne, so yes."

Victoria checked her phone again, finishing the last of her wine.

"Are you waiting for someone else?" Britton asked.

"As a matter of fact, I have a date."

Britton raised an eyebrow. "What if I'd wanted to heat up the sheets for old time's sake?"

Victoria laughed. "I would've loved it, but I know better than that. I've seen you two together, remember, sickeningly sweet."

Britton laughed and shook her head. "I need to get home anyway. It was nice seeing you," she said standing to hug Victoria. "Take care of yourself."

"You too, love," Victoria said, kissing her cheek. "If that little blonde breaks your heart or you remember where you put the real Britton…look me up." She winked.

Britton smiled and walked out of the restaurant.

Chapter 18

Midmorning on Saturday, Britton parked her car in the small driveway next to Daphne's Mercedes and walked up to the door with a big smile on her face. She knocked once and waited only a few seconds for Daphne to pull the door open and fly into her arms.

"I missed you so much!" Daphne said, kissing her passionately.

"You're neighbors are about to see how much," Britton teased, backing her up against the door jam.

Daphne laughed and pushed her back far enough to get them into the house. As soon as the door was shut, Britton pressed Daphne against it, kissing her hard. Daphne melted into the warm body against hers as she wrapped her arms around Britton. Their heated exchange never moved from the door as Britton ran her hand under Daphne's t-shirt, caressing the delicately smooth skin of her abdomen and drifting lower to the waistband of her sweatpants.

Daphne pulled Britton's hand away. "As much as I want you right now, we'd be in bed all weekend and we have way too much to do," she said.

"What?" Britton pulled back slightly, looking into Daphne's sparkling green eyes. "I thought your weekend was free?"

"It is…I'm not going anywhere, but we still have a bunch of last minute wedding stuff to get finished." Daphne stepped away. "Did you get your ring and the marriage certificate?" she asked, walking over to the couch.

"Can't we just spend one day together without talking about the wedding?" Britton sighed, turning to see the coffee table full of catalogs and papers, and Daphne's laptop sitting on the couch with a wedding page opened on the internet.

"We are spending the day together, working on this last minute stuff. My mother sent over the guest list from my side yesterday and your mom is supposed to email me this morning with hers so you and I can get the table arrangements finished. I was thinking you work on your family and I'll work on mine and anyone we can't sit with our family, we put at a mixed table."

"We need to do this right now? The wedding is four weeks away."

"Yes, Britton, we do. We also need to decide on the table setting and figure out if we're using my family's minister or yours, and book the rehearsal dinner."

Britton felt like she was in another world, floating above reality as Daphne went on and on about her plans for the day and the checklist they needed to finish. She wished she could rewind time and arrive at Daphne's door again, before either of them mentioned the word wedding.

"Did you hear me?" Daphne asked, bringing Britton back to reality. "I said I started working on my family's tables last night, so I'm about halfway through them."

"Didn't you work late last night?" Britton asked.

Brides

"Not as late as I thought, so I went ahead and started working on the tables. What did you do last night?"

"I went to C'est la Vie for a drink after work and spent the rest of the night at home, thinking you were working late."

"I haven't been to C'est la Vie in a while. They have the best French cuisine," Daphne stated. "Did you go with Heather?" she asked, shuffling some of the papers on the table.

"No, actually, I met Victoria there."

"What?" Daphne retorted, turning around to face her. "Why would you meet her for a drink?"

"She saw the announcement in the paper and contacted me."

"I'm still not understanding why you met with her." Daphne raise an eyebrow, waiting for a response.

"It wasn't a big deal. We had a couple of glasses of wine and talked." Britton shrugged.

"So, while I was up late working on the guest list for our wedding, you were out on a date with your ex," Daphne spat.

"I didn't know you were working on wedding stuff, you told me you were working late and had the weekend free. How was I to know you had all of this wedding shit to do? I needed a break. It was a long work week and I'm up to my wits end with this wedding, so yes, when she invited me out, I went!" Britton growled.

"Why is it so hard to get you to do things for the wedding? I bet you didn't even get your ring yet! Do you even want to get married, Britton? It's starting to feel like you're just doing this to please everyone else!"

"You're right. I didn't want all of this!" Britton said loudly, losing the last of her patience and letting the frustration of being in a pressure cooker drive her over the edge.

"Then why the hell did you ask me to marry you?"

"I wanted you, Daphne, not the flower colors, maid of honors, flute glasses, table settings, food lists, thank you cards, and all of that other shit!" Britton snapped.

"This is what a wedding is!" Daphne yelled. "If this isn't what you want then you better tell me right now!"

"This..." Britton waved her hands over the table full of crap. "Is not what I want!" Britton shouted back. "It's what everyone else wanted, so I gave it to them!"

"What do you mean everyone else?"

"Daphne, we haven't even been together a year. We don't even live in the same damn state. Didn't you find it a little odd that we got engaged then literally planned a wedding for seven weeks later! Did it ever occur to you that everyone around us, pushed us into this?!"

"Are you saying you only proposed to me because our friends and family pressured you into it?! That's a really weak thing to say to me, Britton!"

Britton ran her hand through her hair in frustration. "I don't know...I guess I am," she said, throwing her hands up.

Daphne wiped a tear from her cheek. "I don't know what to say to you."

Britton stormed out of the townhouse and drove away with the tires squealing on her sports car. The world around her had become a chaotic storm, swirling viciously around her for the past month and she'd just set off a bomb at the very center, disintegrating the entire storm and all of its surroundings. She wiped the tears away as she drove too fast along the interstate.

Brides

~

Unsure of where she was even going, Britton kept driving until the pain burning deep inside and the ache in her chest subsided enough for her to think rationally. She was nearly out of gas when she saw the sign for Westerly and Watch Hill off of US1. Coasting into the nearest gas station, she noticed the signs for Watch Hill Carousel and Beach and Watch Hill Point.

She asked the attendant how much further the point was and he gave her directions to go down Shore Road to Westerly Road to Bluff Road and she'd run directly into it in about another eight miles. So, she paid the bill and headed back out on the road. Driving with the radio blaring and her mind on autopilot, she almost missed the sign for Westerly Road and quickly turned off at the last minute. She had no idea where was going, but had a feeling she'd know when she got there. Sure enough, she turned down the next road and saw the most beautiful Victorian style cottage houses she'd ever seen sitting beach front on the corner and tucked away from everything else in the area. A sign out front had the words Private Cottage Rentals written on it. She pulled into the circular drive and cut the engine off.

The pristine salt air tickled her nose as she got out of her car and walked inside the main house. The décor inside was like stepping into the eighteenth century with modern amenities. A frail, older man walked up to her, pushing his glasses up on his nose and holding his hand out. He was bald on the top and had a small tuft of gray hair on both sides of his head above his ears.

"Welcome to Watch Hill Manor. How may I be of assistance to you?"

Britton eyed him up and down, deciding he looked a lot like Mr. Burns from the Simpson's only he seemed much nicer.

"I saw the sign out front about the rentals," she stated.

"Yes," he smiled. "We have suites and signature cottages available. We have a two night minimum and a weekly rate as well."

Britton nodded. She hadn't planned on staying the night anywhere but Daphne's and now, here she was over an hour and a half away, inquiring about a private beach cottage.

"Two nights it is then." She smiled, handing him her credit card.

"Will that be a suite or a signature suite cottage, Ms. Prescott?" he asked, looking at the name on the card.

"The most private cottage you have would be great," she replied.

The man nodded and smacked the top of a bell that seemed as old as the house. A younger gentleman appeared, looking much like Mr. Smithers. Britton raised an eyebrow.

"Ms. Prescott would like the Sea Gate Cottage for tonight and tomorrow night," the older gentleman informed him, before leaving the room.

"Did my father explain the rates and amenities to you?"

"No."

"I apologize. He's getting up there in years and forgets some things. Watch Hill Manor was built in 1798 and has been in our family since that time. Our ancestors were some of the first settlers to the Westerly and Watch Hill areas. In the mid 1900s this Manor was turned into a

Brides

bed and breakfast. The rooms were made into suites and the cottages that were used for the house staff, became private signature cottages. They were professionally redecorated and upgraded with modern amenities, such as cable TV, internet, glass showers, soaking tubs, efficient kitchenettes, tile or hardwood floors, and air conditioning and heating units. We have a full dining room that serves breakfast, lunch, and dinner at an additional price per guest, per day. We also have a full bar that is open from noon until eleven p.m. The cottages have fully stocked liquor cabinets and wine racks for your convenience, and anything from the bar is available through room service." He handed her a brochure with pictures and pricing.

All Britton wanted to do was crawl into a hole and remember how to breathe again. She'd hoped this little impromptu stay away from town would help clear her head of the tangled wedding web that had cut off the circulation of her life. She quickly signed the paper and grabbed the key as soon as he was finished explaining how to get to her cottage. She walked out to her car and moved it to the side lot, away from the main house and took the cobblestone path down towards the last white-washed building near the cliff that overlooked the rocky beach ten feet below. This cottage was the only one with a private path down to the beach as well. The other three used the main path from the house.

Britton walked inside, noticing the spectacular ocean views from the floor to ceiling windows. French doors opened onto a private terrace with a small seating area and two lounge chairs, while the kitchenette looked into a stunning living room with panoramic views of the Atlantic. It was decorated in ocean style décor with seashells and sand dollars, light hardwood floors and white walls. The living room furniture and matching bar were white-washed oak with blue and white hues. The bedroom had a white-washed oak, king-sized sleigh bed with a matching dresser and the bathroom had a standing shower with a beach-stone floor and a deep-soaking tub.

She set her overnight bag, which she'd packed for a weekend stay at Daphne's house, on the couch and walked over to the kitchenette where the complimentary bottle of wine was chilling in the ice bucket on the bar. Walking around the backside of the bar on the kitchenette side, she noticed the full wine rack and next to it was a cabinet full of minis, pints, and full bottles of the most popular liquor brands.

She grabbed a couple of Blanton's Original Bourbon minis, tossed a few ice cubes into a rocks glass and poured them over the ice, before kicking her shoes off and walking out onto the terrace. The beautiful view was bittersweet. Tears rolled down her face as she leaned against the rail and took a long swallow of the golden liquid. Thinking of the way she'd single-handedly ruined her life, left her knees weak. The bourbon coated her empty stomach, making her want to hurl, but she trudge on, finishing the glass in a couple of long sips.

"How the hell did everything become such a mess?" she said to no one, as she walked inside and poured another round she tried to think back to the point when she'd finally succumbed to the pressure of the world around her and allowed it to cave in, nearly smothering her to death. Everything had happened so quickly. One minute, she and Daphne hated each other, the next they were sleeping together. Then, they were madly in love and out to the world. In a blink of an eye, they were engaged and literally running down the aisle.

Brides

She opened her bag, removed the velvet ring box from the side pocket and opened it, revealing the platinum gold band with a recessed row of nine diamonds, five were white with four blue diamonds in between them. The platinum and white diamond band that matched Daphne's ring was tucked into the box with it, since she'd had it with her to match up. She wiped tears from her eyes as she slid the new ring onto her finger.

~

Day turned into night as Britton sat on the couch, staring out at the sea, drowning her sorrows and sorting through the thoughts racing around her head. She'd never expected things to get so out of hand. Maybe it was for the best. She'd never wanted to get married anyway. She was starting to feel the weight of the world lift off of her shoulders, either that or the alcohol was making her feel weightless. Either way, she felt some relief from the pressure cooker she'd been living in.

The next morning, Britton was sitting on the terrace when the sun began to rise over the ocean. The dawning of that new day was one of the most beautiful things she'd ever seen. Her head pounded and her stomach rumbled like an old locomotive, but none of that mattered as the colors of the world changed in front of her very eyes. The various shades of orange, blue, and pink looked like they were delicately smeared by the brush of an artist. She wiped away the tears rolling down her cheeks. The tears were a mixture of beauty for the sight she was witnessing, sadness for being alone, relief from the pressure around her, heartache from the broken heart she'd caused herself and Daphne, and understanding that she may have ruined the best thing that had ever happened to her. They fell from her eyes, washing over her face until she was all cried out. She finally closed her eyes and let sleep claim her tired body and dreams mend her broken mind.

~

Britton woke up Sunday evening to the sound of waves crashing below and seagulls flying overhead. She was sure she'd fallen asleep out on the terrace and wasn't sure how'd she'd ended up in the bed, but either way, she was thankful for the comfort that allowed her to rest her weary head. Noticing the ring on her left hand, she removed it, storing it safely in its box, and quickly packed up her bag, which hadn't really been opened, before heading out to her car. She was nervous about what she might be coming to home to since she'd turned her phone off the minute she'd left Daphne's house and still hadn't turned it back on, but nevertheless, she put the car in gear and drove towards the interstate. She felt a little lighter from the relief of letting go, but she was still broken on the inside.

Chapter 19

Britton sat in her office on Monday feeling like a completely different person. It was like she physically existed, but mentally she was miles away. She wondered when that feeling of emptiness would subside. The day crawled by, with the second hand moving like the hour hand on the clock in her office. After answering her list of mundane emails, she went to work on the preliminary sketches for the bar, but nothing looked right. The lines were off and the shadows didn't match.

Frustrated from being unable to concentrate, Britton tossed the pencil against the wall and swiped the papers to the floor. She was about to lose her mind when the phone on her desk rang loudly, meaning a call had been transferred to her. She contemplated yelling at Jenna for sending her a call when she clearly didn't feel like talking to anyone. Maybe she should've just stayed home, or better yet, stayed at the cottage where life didn't revolve around a schedule or a plan.

"Britton Prescott," she finally answered.

"Oh, thank God, I was beginning to think you really had gone off the deep end!" Heather exclaimed. "Why haven't you answered any of my calls?"

"What calls?" Britton blew out a frustrating breath and shook her head. She knew better than to answer the phone.

"What calls?! Britton, I've called you a hundred damn times and drove by your house all weekend!"

"My phone is off and I wasn't home."

"No shit! What the hell is going on?"

"It sounds like you already know," Britton sighed. "I'm at work. Can we talk about this another time?"

"I'm coming over after work," Heather declared, sounding like a cat on catnip.

"I'll be there," Britton replied, before hanging up the phone.

~

At five o'clock, Britton silently prayed for a last minute meeting or another work-related issue to come up to keep her from going home and having the conversation she'd been dreading since leaving the cottage, but the phone never rang. She was the last to leave behind Jenna and Kathleen. Locking the door, she looked up at the sky and sighed before getting into her car.

The drive to her apartment from downtown seemed shorter than normal. She wondered if maybe it was her mind playing tricks on her as she pulled into her parking space and cut the engine.

As soon as Britton kicked off her shoes and shed her pantsuit, the doorbell rang. She pulled on an old pair of sweatpants and a t-shirt and padded across the apartment to open the door.

"You look like hell," Heather muttered, pushing her way inside.

Brides

"Thanks, you look great too," Britton sneered, closing the door.

"Britt—"

"Can we at least open that first?" Britton interjected, looking down at the bottle of red wine Heather was holding. Walking into the kitchen, she fished through the cabinets for a pair of glasses and pulled the corkscrew from the drawer.

Heather set the wine on the dining table and sat down in one of the chairs. Britton walked over, opening the bottle easily and pouring two glasses, before sitting down adjacent to her.

"I don't even know where to start," Britton sighed, drinking from her glass.

"How about the beginning? Bridget called me flipping out and saying you and Daphne split up. What the hell happened?"

"It's a lot more complicated than that." Britton's eyes met her best friend's. "I couldn't take the pressure anymore."

"Pressure of what? Getting married? That's all part of the experience. It's a chaotic cluster fuck until you wake up on the honeymoon." Heather sipped her wine. "I talked to Daphne yesterday. She said you told her you were pressured into marrying her."

"I was." Britton shrugged. "My family didn't give me an ultimatum, but they pretty much put the ring in my hand and set the date. Hell, I was getting it from everyone, you included. All I kept hearing was get engaged, get engaged, get engaged. Then, I do it, and within hours it's get married, get married, get married. The date was set and the invitations were ordered before it even settled in that I'd actually asked her to marry me."

"It did happen fast, but I thought that's what you wanted."

Britton finished her glass of wine and slid it towards the center of the table. "I never wanted to get married, Heather."

"Then why did you do any of this?"

"Because, it was the next step or at least that's what everyone kept telling me. I love Daphne and this is something she wants. It's not the getting married part that is driving me crazy, I've come to terms with getting married and spending the rest of my life with one person because that person is her, but it's all of this other shit that goes with it. The planning this and doing that and deadlines here and last minute things there. I felt like I was a damn pressure cooker and I couldn't take it anymore. I shouldn't feel like that. Getting married to the person I'm in love with should be the happiest time of my life, not the honest to god worst. I've been miserable for weeks, Heather. Weeks!"

"Why the hell didn't you say anything to anyone?"

"Every time I did, everyone just said this was normal and wedding planning is crazy and then it's all over. Well, I don't want it at all if it has to be like this."

Heather sympathized with her best friend. She'd rarely ever seen Britton so distraught. "What do you want?" Heather asked, pouring Britton another glass.

"I wanted to be engaged for at least a year. I wanted a small, intimate ceremony, we both did actually. I wanted…hell, I wanted anything, but this scripted stage production that's being put together." Britton sipped her wine. "This isn't me, Heather. I'm not the Prescott that showboats everywhere she goes and with everything she does. It's my last name and it's my family, but it's not me."

"Have you told you mother any of this?"

"Have you met my mother?!" Britton retorted. "Daphne's mother hasn't been a cakewalk either. Between the two of them, my damn head is constantly spinning and Daphne seems fine hopping all over the place like a rabbit on speed, but you know me better than that."

"Yeah." Heather grinned. "You definitely move at your own pace and to the beat of your own drum."

Britton raised an eyebrow.

"Have you talked about any of this with Daphne?"

"I can't. All she talks about is wedding this and wedding that. The only time she calls me anymore is to see if I did this or ask me to do that or get snappy with me because I haven't done something else. Hell, Saturday was the first time I'd seen her in nearly three weeks." She ran her hand through her hair, pushing it back out of her face and over her shoulders. "I lost contact with the person I was in love with and the reality I lived in. It's like everyone was on autopilot around me."

"You have to communicate, Britton. Daphne won't know how you feel unless you tell her." Heather refilled her own glass. "When I heard Victoria's name I wanted to choke the life out of you. What was that all about?"

Britton rolled her eyes. "She saw the damn ad in the paper and wanted to meet for a drink to tell me congratulations. We talked for a little bit, drank some wine, and I left because she was meeting a date. I told Daphne where I was because she asked what I did Friday night and she lost her shit. Trust me, Victoria is history. I'd screw a fat, hairy dude, before getting with her again."

Heather scrunched her face.

"She actually told me she'd seen Daphne and me a while back and it was sickening how in love we were."

"Well, I have to agree with her on that one. If there were ever two people that were so meant for each other it's ridiculous... it's you and Daphne. You're madly in love with each other, Britt. There's no way it's over, neither of you would give in this easily. You two are the most headstrong people I've ever met in my entire life. That's probably the reason you spent so many years hating and loving each other at the same time. Hell, maybe that's why your sex life is so damn explosive." She shrugged.

Britton grinned.

"Going slightly off topic for a second, where were you all weekend?"

"Down the coast, near the Connecticut border and on the ocean."

"What was down there?"

"A beautiful beach cottage. I needed to be as far away from everyone and everything as I could possibly get. I had to clear the web that was suffocating my brain."

"Were you alone?"

Britton cocked her head to the side and raised an eyebrow. "You're my best friend. I honestly can't believe you just asked me that. Yes, of course I was alone. I cried my eyes out and drowned my sorrow in a bottle of bourbon all weekend. The fresh air and change of scenery was good. It helped me see a lot of things more clearly."

"Why couldn't you have done that at home?"

"Honestly, I got in the car and I drove until I literally ran out of gas. I didn't want to go home, so I took a different route and wound up down at the bottom of the state near the coast. I knew you and my family would be

Brides

looking for me and I just wasn't ready to talk. I needed to take a couple of days to find myself again," Britton sighed. "Haven't you ever felt like that? Like you needed to escape reality in order to get back in control of your life?"

Heather shrugged. "No. I guess I've never really been to the breaking point."

"It's not a nice place," Britton replied.

"What are you going to do now?" Heather asked.

"I don't know."

"Well, I think you and Daphne need to talk."

"I don't think either of us are ready for that right now."

"Maybe Daphne needs fresh air and a change of scenery too. You've both been running around like headless chickens and you need to take some time to find yourselves again. Find that spark that brought you together and the reason you asked her to marry you in the first place." Heather held up her hand. "I don't care what anyone was saying to you. I know you, Britton, and I know you don't do anything irrationally, so if you proposed to her, then you did it because you meant it and because you love her."

Britton bent over, pressing her forehead against the table. Her hair fell over the sides of her face.

"You know I'm right, now wrap up this pity party, get over the mountain you seem to think is in front of you and do what's in your heart. To hell with everyone and everything else. All that matters should be the two of you. If you let things come between you now, it will happen throughout your entire lives and your marriage will never work."

"When did you get so philosophical and smart?"

"You ass!" Heather laughed. "It took a lot of soul searching for me to get married. Sure, I love Greg, but after seeing what my parents went through, then divorcing, and eventually remarrying, I just didn't want that for myself. So, I made sure this was what I wanted and I vowed to work damn hard to make sure nothing and no one ever comes between us."

"I love you, you know that right?"

"Yeah, and I love you too, which is why I'm over here making sure you don't make the biggest mistake of your life. I'll smack you over the head with a large board if that's what it takes."

"Thanks," Britton grinned. "I need a little more time, but I promise I'll talk to her," she sighed, knowing Heather was right.

Chapter 20

Britton was sitting in her office Tuesday morning, looking over the new permits she'd received for the library. She had a dozen phone calls to make in order to schedule the construction crew and prepare for the ground breaking. The last thing she wanted to do was talk to her sister, so she wanted to scream when the phone on her desk rang and she snatched it up, not thinking who would be on the other end.

"I cannot believe what you've done. Have you lost your mind?" Bridget spat.

"Calm down, Bridget, before your eyes bug out of your head. You don't know the whole story," Britton retorted.

"What am I missing? You broke Daphne's heart and confused the hell out of me. Where the hell were you all weekend? If you say Victoria's I'm going to drive over there and slap you myself."

"Bridget, I love Daphne with all of my heart. I wasn't with anyone. I drove out of town to try and clear my head."

"What has you so mixed up that you've lost your mind?"

Britton sighed. "It's a long story."

"I'm on my lunch break," Bridget replied.

"Oh, for crying out loud, Bridget. I have work to do."

"Either you talk to me, or I'm going to mom and dad, whom I haven't told yet, by the way."

"Threatening me with mom and dad isn't going to work anymore. I'm twenty-five years old!"

"Fine. I'll see if they can get you to talk then—"

"Wait!" Britton yelled. "Damn it, Bridget, you're such a pain in my ass!" she spat as she got up and shut her office door.

"I'll have you know, Daphne is my best friend and I've never seen her like this."

"Well, I'm your sister, blood is thicker than water and all of that. Or has that thought never occurred to you?"

"Oh, get on with it already."

"I don't know what to tell you, other than I was severely overwhelmed with all of this wedding stuff. It's not me, Bridge. I never wanted a huge wedding with all of this pomp and circumstance. I love Daphne with all of my heart, but I had to take a minute and breathe before I suffocated."

"Have you said any of this to her?"

"No, that's just it, we've barely talked at all since we got engaged! It's been wedding this and planning that."

Bridget sighed. "Well, you sure as hell have her attention now. Doing what you did wasn't the best way to get it either. I know things are happening very fast for you two, but you need to take the time to communicate and that goes both ways."

"I know. You sound like Heather." Britton ran her hand through her hair, pushing it back over her shoulder. "Don't say anything to Daphne. I need to do this myself."

Brides

"Well, you better straighten this out soon. The invitations have already been mailed and—"

"You see, that's exactly my point! Here we go again with all lists of this and that." Britton blew out a frustrating breath. "I'll talk to her, just keep your mouth closed about all of this," Britton said before hanging up.

~

The next two days went by in a blur of emails, phone calls, and drawings until she was too tired to look at her drawing desk any longer. She walked into her apartment, laid her briefcase on the table and ran herself a hot bath full of bubbles. Knowing the delivery place around the corner would take forever to get her order delivered to her, she went ahead and called in her dinner before getting into the tub.

The hot water relaxed her muscles, as well as her tired brain. Her mind drifted off to the last time she'd taken a bubble bath and she smiled, remembering how good it had felt to hold Daphne in her arms and how cute she'd looked covered in bubbles. They'd made love on the floor of the bathroom that night because they couldn't wait the second and a half it took to reach Britton's bed.

As a tear rolled down Britton's cheek, she wiped it away, realizing the best times of her life were more than likely behind her if she didn't find a way to balance the chaos of work, life, and everything that went with it, including the fairytale wedding that was supposed to take place in three weeks. She quickly got out of the tub and dried off, looking at the bags under her eyes in the mirror as she brushed her teeth and washed her face.

A few minutes later, Britton forgot about her ordered dinner as she dressed in a pair of jeans and a sweater and rushed out to her car. She drove the forty minute drive on autopilot. She knew wasn't thinking rationally, it was the middle of the week and nearly eight o'clock at night.

Despite her initial gut feeling to turn around, she kept driving and arrived at Daphne's house, happy to see her car in the driveway. She got out and knocked, waited, then knocked again, wondering if maybe she'd made a huge mistake.

"Hi," Daphne said, finally answering the door.

"Hey," Britton replied, sounding more defeated than she'd meant to. Seeing Daphne's face was like a blow to the chest with a sledgehammer. "I really want to talk to you, about a lot of things, but I didn't want to do it over the phone."

"Okay?" Daphne waited, reluctant to let her in out of the cold.

Britton had forgotten her jacket, so she crossed her arms to fend off the cool air blowing around her. "I don't know where to start."

"How about the beginning?" Daphne murmured, swallowing the lump in her throat and pushing the door open further. Seeing Britton was difficult, but watching her shiver in the cold was too much to bear.

Britton walked inside. The coffee table and couch were void of the wedding stuff that had covered them the last time she'd stood in the spot. Daphne sat down and waved for her to do the same.

Britton didn't know what else to do, so she simply let it all out. "My mother had been pushing me to marry you since the day after she caught us in bed together. So many people hounded me over and over about getting engaged and getting married," she paused. "I love you, Daphne, with all of my heart, so I decided to take the next step and I asked you to marry me."

She looked up, meeting Daphne's green eyes. "That was one of the happiest moments in my life. However, I did not expect my mom to have the date booked within a week and the ceremony scheduled to take place in less than two months! It was way too much at one time," she sighed. "I needed to slow down and breathe for a minute. I didn't mean to hurt you. I simply couldn't take it anymore. I felt like my life was no longer mine and everyone was pulling me in all of these directions like a puppet on a string. I never meant for things to get so out of hand. I'm partly to blame for allowing everything to get to me the way it did."

Daphne wiped the tears from her eyes. "I don't understand, Britton. Why did you let them manipulate you like that? You're the strongest person I know." She shook her head. "I should've known something was wrong. I thought you were being negative about everything because you're not into party planning and other…I don't know…girly things, I guess is the right word." She wiped a few more tears. "Getting married because everyone else wants us to, is not a reason to get married at all."

Britton wiped a few of her own tears, shaking her head. "Daphne, I want to spend the rest of my life with you, and that involves getting married. It's not the marriage thing that has my head spinning, it's all of the planning and chaos that is going into this last minute stage performance everyone is calling a wedding. It's way over the top and way more than I ever intended."

Daphne nodded. "It is a little extreme, I agree."

"I know my family has ties and a big name in this state, but that's all it is to me. It's a name. It's not who I am and it doesn't define me. You know me better than that. Did you honestly think three hundred guests, black tie only, fancy china patterns, a five star specialty cuisine, and a huge newspaper announcement, sounded like something I'd be interested in?"

Daphne shrugged. "I knew you wanted a long engagement and a small ceremony, but I assumed you were going along with everything your mother had planned, so I went with what mine wanted to do."

"That's just it, you assumed things and I assumed things and we never communicated. Hell, we barely spoke except for reminders to do this and that." Britton shook her head. "I wanted to marry you because I love you and this should be one of the happiest times in our lives."

"I agree. I love you too, so much that the thought of losing you scares me to death. I want you to be happy about getting married."

Britton leaned over, kissing Daphne's lips softly. Pulling back, she looked into her eyes and whispered, "Go away with me this weekend."

"What?" Daphne asked.

"Let's get out of here, away from everyone and away from that damn wedding, and remember why I asked you and why you said yes in the first place."

"I don't know. I have a lot of—"

"If you say wedding stuff, I'm walking out that door and I'm not coming back. We need this, Daphne. I need you, and only you. No phones, no emails, no magazine clippings, no deadlines, no checklists, no parents, just us, you and me."

Brides

"Where do you want to go?" Daphne sighed, looking into the beautiful gray eyes in front of her.

"I don't know. Somewhere they can't find us would be a great start. Maybe somewhere tranquil, where the clock ticks a little slower than everywhere else."

"That sounds like a fairytale place."

"When I took off to clear my head, I wound up driving down the coast and ended up in a little town and stayed in a beautiful beachfront cottage."

"Why don't we go there? Or is it a bad memory?"

"No, well, it's someplace you'd love and it actually made me miss you even more."

"Hmm…" Daphne thought for a second, then smiled. "I think forgetting about everything for a few days is a great idea," she said, kissing Britton softly.

"Great, we'll go there then. Can you leave in the morning?"

"I have a few things to do in the morning, but how about lunchtime?"

"That works for me. We'll leave from my apartment. I'll call in the morning and make the reservation."

Chapter 21

Daphne watched the gorgeous scenery go by as they rode through the small beach towns on the way to their destination. When Britton turned into the parking lot of the large Victorian house, Daphne smiled.

"How old is this house?" she whispered.

"Old," Britton grinned. "Come on."

Nothing had changed in the week since Britton had last stepped foot into the large manor, except, now she was where she was meant to be, with the person she was meant to share that place with.

"It's nice to see you again, Ms. Prescott," Smithers said. Britton didn't know his name and had taken to calling him Smithers. "We have the Sea Gate Cottage ready as requested." He handed her the key and slid the papers to her to sign.

"I didn't get to explore last time I was here. Are there any shops or restaurants within walking distance?" Britton asked.

"Yes, ma'am. If you go up the main road to the right and take the first left, you will find a street full of small family owned shops and a few restaurants and further down is a small museum, the historic courthouse, which we still use today, and a few treasures. This time of year it's very quaint and easy to get around on foot."

Brides

"Thank you," she said, grabbing the key and nodding for Daphne to follow her out.

They moved the car and carried their bags down to the cottage. The crisp, cool ocean air was tinged with the scent of salt and sand.

"Wow, can we live here?" Daphne exclaimed, looking at the view and taking in the scenery and décor around her. "This place is perfect."

Britton raised an eyebrow. "You do remember the beachfront house we're in the process of building, don't you?"

"Yes, of course, it's huge. This place is quaint and cozy. I don't know why, but I really like it."

"It's a little too late to change the design of our house, especially since the walls are up."

"They are?" Daphne squealed.

"Yes. I was by there a few days ago. It'll be done in about a month."

"I can't wait to move in."

"I thought you wanted quaint and cozy?" Britton teased, wrapping her arms around her. She wasn't sure how far she should go since they were still trying to get back on comfortable footing around each other.

"I said, I liked this place because it was quaint and cozy. It's very tranquil, but I love that mansion you're building us. Are you kidding me, it's big enough to put my townhouse into it about fifteen times!" Daphne exclaimed, kissing her softly.

Britton laughed. "It's hardly a mansion."

"It's costing two million dollars!"

"More like three, but who's counting," Britton teased. "It's still smaller than my parents' estate. They lose each other in there sometimes."

"No, thank you. I never want a house so large that I can't find you." Daphne shook her head. "I remember the house they lived in when I first met you and Bridget. That one was pretty large too."

"Yeah, that was the house we grew up in. I guess the square footage is probably close in size to the one we're building." Britton pulled away. Grabbing Daphne's hand, she tugged her along as she walked out onto the terrace.

Daphne took a deep breath, and stepped up to the rail, watching the waves crash against the rocky shore below.

"I love you so damn much," Britton said, sliding up behind her and slipping her arms around Daphne's waist.

"I love you too," Daphne replied, placing her head back on Britton's shoulder. "I've missed you like crazy."

"I'm so sorry. I don't want to ever go through anything like that ever again. From this moment on, I promise to communicate with you about everything, whether we agree or not. I promise to always be there for you and allow you to be there for me."

Daphne turned in Britton's arms.

"Above all, I promise to never ever let you go or push you away again. You make my life complete, Daphne."

"Are those your vows?" Daphne asked, smiling softly.

Britton shrugged lightly. "Maybe they are."

"They're beautiful. I'm sorry too and I vow to do the same you know. I promise to always share everything with you and make decisions with you by my side. I promise to love you no matter what. I have loved you most of my life, Britton and I promise to be by your side and continue loving you for the rest of it."

Brides

Britton wiped the tears from her own eyes with one hand and the tears from Daphne's with the other, before kissing her passionately. Daphne pushed Britton back towards the opened doorway, careful not to break the heated kiss. Britton crossed the threshold and quickly picked Daphne up into her arms, carrying her into the bedroom and depositing her onto the bed.

Clothes were shed before skin met skin as they laid down together, kissing and touching like new lovers, making love for the first time. Britton ran her hand down Daphne's body. Moving over her, Britton bent her head, taking one of Daphne's nipples in her mouth and sucking it tenderly, before moving her head lower.

Daphne anticipated the contact before she felt it. The muscles in her stomach rolled and flopped as Britton's lips trailed warm kisses across it. Dipping lower, Britton looked up at green eyes staring back and softly licked the glistening lips in front of her, one slow stroke at a time, careful not to break eye contact as she watched Daphne's face change with each caress.

"Come here," Daphne whispered huskily, pulling Britton's mouth up to hers. Sharing a passionate kiss, she tasted herself on Britton's lips and pushed her hand between them until she found the spot she was looking for.

Britton lifted her hips slightly, allowing Daphne access as she followed suit, placing her fingers on the spot her mouth had vacated. They traded fervent kisses and delicate moans as they rubbed lazily circles, careful to match each other stroke for stroke.

Daphne pulled back, looking into Britton's eyes as her body tightened. Britton's breath caught in her chest as she forced herself to concentrate as the wave of pleasure tore through her like a hot-edged blade. Daphne cried out and Britton moaned like a caged animal as they came together with their bodies quivering and thrashing together.

"Oh my God," Britton gasped, rolling off Daphne and onto her back.

Daphne rolled her head to the side, grinning at her. "You're so beautiful."

"Marry me," Britton said, looking at her eyes.

Daphne smiled. "You've already asked me that," she replied, holding her hand up, revealing the shimmering ring in the late afternoon sunlight that was pouring in through the uncovered windows.

"I mean here…now," Britton murmured.

"What about our parents and the huge wedding we have planned?"

"Daphne, I almost lost you over that huge wedding. This…right here and now…this is us; tranquil and simple, not a well orchestrated cluster fuck that pleases our parents." She ran her hand through her hair. "I'm so damn sick of having to skirt egg shells because nothing I do pleases my parents. Well, to hell with them. I'm grown and I'll do things the way I want to do them and I want to marry you right here and right now."

"Who are you and what have you done with my girlfriend?" Daphne smiled. "I love you more than life…yes…yes, I'll marry you right here and now. Yes!" She squealed.

Britton leaned over, kissing her passionately and rolling Daphne on top of her. Pulling away, Daphne sat up.

"What are we going to wear? What about our rings and—"

Brides

Britton silenced her with another long kiss, then said, "We'll figure it out along the way."

They both tore through their suitcases. Britton pulled on a light colored pair of jeans and a light gray oxford style shirt with a white v-neck sweater over it. The collar was opened wide, and the sleeves were rolled back a little bit with the cuff of the oxford shirt over the sweater. She bent over, shaking her hair, before flipping it back over her shoulders.

Daphne's mouth watered.

"What?" Britton raised an eyebrow, cocking her head to the side. "Do I look okay? I know it's not ideal—"

"You're sexy as hell," Daphne murmured, biting her bottom lip.

"Hold that thought and get dressed before I ravish your body right here on this floor," Britton replied, kissing her cheek and backing away to keep her distance.

She walked into the living room while Daphne continued searching for something to wear and remembered the rings were still in her briefcase because she'd forgotten about them. She quickly dug through it, pulled the box out, and slipped the rings into the front pocket of her jeans. She was about to close the briefcase when she it dawned on her that they'd need their birth certificates. She quickly flipped through the files until she found the one that had both of their birth certificates. She'd had them with her so she could get the marriage license. She'd almost forgotten about being told by the clerk at the courthouse that they both needed to be present, something everyone failed to mention to her, which was why she hadn't obtained the license.

The last thing she did was look up the information on her phone and make a call to the front desk.

"Well, do I look like a blushing bride?" Daphne laughed as she stepped out of the room wearing a light champagne colored, cable-knit sweater dress, with a thin, dark brown belt low on her hips, crème colored stockings and matching dark brown, leather slouch boots that were calf high with no heel.

"Wow," Britton murmured. "I think I'm under dressed."

"No, you look great. This is a casual look, by the way. I bought it when I was out doing registry stuff."

"I definitely like it," Britton said, wrapping her arms around Daphne's waist and kissing her lips. "Are you ready?" she asked.

"To spend the rest of my life with you?" Daphne smiled, kissing her. "I've been ready for a long time," she answered.

"Then, let's go." Britton grabbed her hand, interlacing their fingers.

"Wait, don't we need stuff?"

"I have the rings, our birth certificates and our ID's. Sorry, I went in your purse without asking, by the way. I've got cash and my credit card. Do we need anything else?"

"No, I guess not."

As they walked down to the car, Britton said, "I Googled the courthouse. It's up the street. We'll drive so we can get there quicker. They close in half an hour. Once we get the license, pretty much any judge or minister can do the ceremony and I have some more good news."

"What's that?"

"Mr. Burns happens to be a former district court judge, so he can perform the ceremony and his son and

Brides

daughter-in-law, who run this place, can be our witnesses. So, all we have to do is go get the license and they will meet us down on the beach."

"Wow. You were busy while I was getting dressed. I didn't think it took me that long."

"It didn't." Britton smiled. "I'm just efficient."

~

There was no line at the town clerk's office when they arrived and as soon as they walked in, a man in a uniform locked the doors behind them, indicating the office was closed for the day. Britton breathed a sigh of relief as they stepped up to the window.

It took all of five minutes for Daphne and Britton to get the registration completed and sign the papers. A minute later, the woman behind the counter slid the marriage license across the counter and told them congratulations. Both women were slightly giddy as they got back in the car.

After a quick stop at the tiniest florist shop they'd ever seen, they arrived back at the manor, where Mr. Burns, whom Britton had found out was the retired, Honorable Chief Justice Franklin Blackstock, was standing on the beach with a large black book in his hand. His son, Maurice Blackstock, whom she'd been referring to as Smithers, was next to him and Maurice's wife, Amy, who had a camera dangling around her neck, was standing off to the side.

"Are you ready?" Britton grinned, lightly shivering, more from the cool air than from being nervous.

"Absolutely," Daphne said, smiling brightly.

Graysen Morgen

The sun sank a little lower on the horizon and Daphne squeezed the small bouquet of blue and white flowers in her hand and laced her arm through Britton's. The click of the camera and the crashing of the waves was the only sound heard as they walked down the beach stone path that had been laid out for them as a makeshift aisle.

Judge Blackstock opened the book in his hands and spoke loudly to be heard over the nearby waves.

"On this day, you give your hearts to each other in a promise to be faithful and supportive, to communicate fully and fearlessly, to love each other unconditionally through sickness and in health, and to make each other's weaknesses your strengths. Above all, you promise to laugh together, cry together, and respect and cherish your undying love for each other." Looking up from the book, he asked," Britton, do you vow here today, in front of the witnesses, to make this solemn promise to Daphne in the binding commitment of this marriage?"

Britton inhaled slowly and turned to look at the green eyes staring back at her. "Yes, I do."

Daphne smiled softly as she let out the breath she'd been holding.

The judge continued. "Daphne, do you vow here today, in front of the witnesses, to make this solemn promise to Britton in the binding commitment of this marriage?"

"Yes, I do."

"Do we have rings?" he asked, looking from one to the other.

"Oh, uh—" Daphne started.

"Right here," Britton said, pulling them from her front pocket. She handed her ring to Daphne and held

Brides

Daphne's ring in her hand. When Daphne raised a questioning eyebrow, Britton simply smiled at her.

"Britton, place the ring on Daphne's left hand and repeat after me: Daphne, this ring is a symbol of my love and solemn promise to you today. As I place it on your finger, I commit my heart and soul to you for the rest of my life."

Britton slid the ring over Daphne's knuckle and repeated the words.

"Daphne, place the ring on Britton's left hand and repeat after me: Britton, this ring is a symbol of my love and solemn promise to you today. As I place it on your finger, I commit my heart and soul to you for the rest of my life."

Daphne pushed the ring onto Britton's finger, then wiped a stray tear from her face as she repeated the words.

"Let it be known, that here today on this, the twenty-first day of the month of November, in the year two thousand and fourteen, Britton and Daphne entered the legal binding commitment of marriage and promised their undying love to each other in front of myself and these witnesses. By the power vested in me by the state of Rhode Island, I hereby pronounce you Britton and Daphne Prescott."

Britton's spine tingled from top to bottom as he said those words.

Judge Blackstock smiled at Daphne and winked at Britton. "It's time to kiss your wife," he exclaimed.

Amy took more pictures while Maurice Blackstock and the judge clapped and cheered as Britton pulled Daphne into her arms, kissing her passionately. Daphne held the flowers in one hand as she wrapped her arms around Britton's neck.

"I love you so damn much," Daphne squealed.

"I love you too, wife!" Britton teased with a huge smile.

Amy took a few more photos and Judge Blackstock cleared his throat, to get everyone's attention. He quickly had everyone sign the marriage certificate, then he placed his signature at the bottom.

"Two bottles of complimentary champagne and a cake will be waiting in your cottage when you return," he said. "It was an honor and privilege to officiate this ceremony for you both. I wish you all the luck and happiness in the world," he added, shaking their hands.

When he was finished, Amy grabbed their attention and took a picture of Britton and Daphne with him, and then had the two of them pose together in different ways for a few more pictures as the sunset behind them cast an orange glow over the beach.

~

After everyone left, Britton and Daphne walked hand in hand down the dimly lit beach, watching the last of the sun slip below the ocean. Britton wrapped her arm around Daphne, pulling her close when the cold evening air caused them both to shiver.

Daphne exhaled deeply, wrapping her arm across Britton's stomach, stopping their progress.

"What was that for?" Britton asked, holding Daphne loosely in her arms.

"I feel like I'm in a dream," Daphne whispered, looking into her eyes.

Brides

Britton held her left hand up. Glancing at the shiny ring, she shook her head. "Definitely not a dream," she smiled.

"As beautiful as the beach is," Daphne paused, kissing her deeply. "I can think of a few much warmer places where we could be wearing a lot less clothing."

"Oh," Britton raised an eyebrow, nibbling on Daphne's lower lip. "I think the way you think, Mrs. Prescott."

Daphne smiled. "I like the way that sounds. Is it really Mrs. or would it just be Ms.?"

Britton shrugged. "I don't know. I didn't change my name. What did your papers say?"

"I don't know. I was so nervous and excited, I rushed through them, signing where she'd marked," Daphne laughed.

Britton shook her head and laughed with her as they started walking back towards the cottage. "Well, I think it's probably Ms. for both of us. I guess we'll find out when we get everything in the mail. What address did you give them?"

"Mine."

Britton smiled. "I bet that looks odd, we have different addresses."

"I'm sure there are people like us that are old fashioned and don't live together before they're married."

"That wasn't by choice and it looks like we'll be married and still not living together." Britton looked up to see the full moon and a number stars in the distance. "Hey, look at that." She pointed. "There isn't a cloud in the sky."

"It's beautiful. What a way to end a perfect day," Daphne smiled.

"Aww, you're a poet. Did you know it?" Britton grinned.

Daphne bumped shoulders with her. "Great. I married a smartass," she laughed.

"I may be smart, but I am not an ass. I'm more like a stallion mixed with a thoroughbred," Britton stated matter-of-factly.

Daphne tried to hold back her laughter. "Does that make me your jockey?"

"Ohhh, that could be fun," Britton murmured, wiggling her eyebrows. "Do you ride bareback?"

Daphne rolled her eyes and smiled as she turned down the private path that led to their cottage, pulling Britton along by their intertwined hands.

~

Britton and Daphne awoke around midmorning on Sunday, sleep deprived, dehydrated, and starving. They'd started their honeymoon in the soaking tub Friday night with the first bottle of champagne and a couple slices of cake, and because they couldn't leave each other alone long enough to get dressed and go somewhere, they'd wound up living off the remaining cake and champagne for the rest of the weekend.

"Do we have to go back?" Britton pouted as she trailed her finger over Daphne's breast and around her peaked nipple. The blue and white diamonds of her wedding band glistened in the sunlight peaking through the closed curtains.

"Unless you want our families to send out a search party, yes," Daphne replied.

Brides

"They're going to be pissed when they find out. We may have just signed a deal with the devil," Britton stated.

"Why do we have to tell them? They wanted this big wedding that's already planned, so why not let them have it? You and I got what we wanted and that's all that matters to us."

"You're right," Britton nodded.

"Are you going to be okay with the chaos when we get home?"

"Yes." Britton smiled, leaning down to kiss her softly. "I've already married you, so this other wedding should be a cake walk. It'll be easier knowing that it's all for them and I already have what I wanted."

"Oh, really? What was it that you wanted?" Daphne asked, rolling Britton onto her back.

"No debating over server setting styles, over the top guest lists, who sits where at what table, perfect flowers, five-star menus or anything else that is all utter nonsense. I wanted to marry you, not perform on stage and host the Whitehouse Correspondents Dinner Party. I wanted you and I standing at the altar, vowing to love each other for the rest of our lives. Simple, but beautiful."

The smile on Daphne's face was full of admiration. "That's why I married you. This is the Britton I fell in love with. The one that doesn't conform and the one who lives her life as who she is, not what she is."

"I'm glad the Daphne I fell in love with joined me on this impromptu trip. I married her because it was perfect and felt right, but I may have drowned the other one who was a frenzied, wedding planning figment of her, had she joined me," Britton stated, kissing Daphne softly.

Daphne giggled, "Come on, we better get back. I'm scared to turn my phone on."

"Did anyone know where you were going?"

"No. I told Bridget you and I had talked and were taking this weekend to get back to where we were before all of the wedding stuff."

"Well, I'm pretty sure we did that." Britton nodded. "And then some," she added with a grin.

"Yeah, we have a new name for reconciliation; it's called marriage," Daphne laughed.

Chapter 22

On Monday morning, Daphne was up early, racing around and getting ready to go to work. She'd stayed the night at Britton's and had nearly an hour long drive to her office. Britton had plenty of time, so she chose to say under the warm sheets a little longer. She propped her head up with her hand and watched Daphne as she dressed.

"I don't like being married and not living together," Britton sighed.

"Yeah, I don't like it either. I was thinking on the way back yesterday, I'm going to ask your father to transfer me to a distribution center in Rhode Island. It may not happen until after the house is ready, but I don't want to be working that far away and in another state to boot."

Britton nodded. "That's if he doesn't fire you," she teased.

"Why would he do that?"

"You just secretly married his daughter," Britton replied, ducking the towel Daphne tossed at her from the bathroom doorway.

"Speaking of that," Daphne said, pulling her wedding set off. She handed the wedding band to Britton and slid her engagement ring back on. "I better leave this with you. I'd be too tempted to wear it."

"You should be wearing it," Britton huffed, removing hers as well.

"In less than two weeks, we will be wearing them for the rest of our lives. I think a few days won't hurt." Daphne leaned down, kissing her lips softly. "I love you and I know I'm married to you. That's all that matters to me."

"I love you too."

"Will I see you tonight?" Daphne asked, putting her shoes on.

"I don't know. I have a shit ton of stuff to do this week and it's a short week with Thanksgiving in a couple of days."

"That's right. I completely forgot it was this week. I'm assuming you'll be with your family and I'll be with mine?"

"Why don't we make an appearance at both houses together, like the married couple we are?"

"That's a great idea, then neither of us will get stuck with our families all day."

"Exactly my point," Britton exclaimed. "I do have to work Friday though."

"Yeah, me too," Daphne replied, leaning down to kiss her again. "I need to get on the road or I'll be late. I love you," she said.

"I love you too. I'll call you later," Britton replied.

~

Britton strolled into her office Tuesday morning with the same grin on her face as the day before. Kathleen and

Jenna looked at her, then at each other with raised eyebrows, but Britton paid them no attention as she sat down at her drawing desk with her notes. Kathleen walked into her office and knocked on the open office door.

"I saw the permits were finalized for the library," Kathleen stated. "Would you like me to pull the construction schedule?"

"No. I'll deal with that next week. I need to get these bar sketches finished by tomorrow. I worked late last night and got most of the outline finished."

"Okay, let me know if you need me to reschedule your meeting with the bar owner."

"That won't be necessary. I should be able to get these finished if I work late again tonight, but if you would go ahead and take my calls so I don't have any interruptions today, and make sure my schedule is open tomorrow, that would be great."

"Sure," Kathleen said with a smile as she left the room and pulled the door closed.

Britton went back to the sketches in front of her. Her left hand looked odd without the ring on it. She never realized how much saying some heartfelt words, putting a piece of jewelry on, and signing a piece of paper would change her life. Physically, she was the same person, but mentally, she felt a little older. So much had changed in just a few days, she was even walking a little taller, or so it seemed.

She knew she was in for another long day and night, but she was cutting her deadline very close. She'd originally planned to work on the bar sketches all day Friday, and then a little bit more over the weekend, but her plans were changed at the last minute. Thinking back on the reason they had changed made her smile again. It also made her miss Daphne. Monday night had been their first night apart since getting married and Britton had tossed and turned for most of it.

~

A few hours later, Britton had finished the exterior sketches and was about to start the interior outline when her cell phone rang. Thinking it could be Daphne, she walked over to her regular desk to retrieve the phone. Heather's smiling face was on the screen.

"Don't you work?" Britton asked, answering the call.

"Yes, smartass. I hadn't heard from you. How did the weekend go?"

"It went fine. We talked about a lot of things and made promises to each other," Britton said nonchalantly.

"That's great. See, I knew once you guys talked, you would figure things out. The wedding's two weeks away from this Saturday and it will all be over with. Then, you and Daphne can move on with your lives."

"Yeah, two more weeks."

"You'll get through it. These last couple of weeks nearly did me in, but I think you'll be fine. Keep telling yourself it's just another day."

Britton smiled. "You know, I have been saying that, especially since this weekend. The upcoming wedding is just another day and I'll let my mom have the party and big to-do that she wants."

"Who are you and what have you done with my best friend?" Heather laughed.

Brides

Britton laughed too. "I don't know. I guess I'm seeing things a lot more clearly now and this wedding planning stuff isn't bothering me anymore."

"Well, that's great. I'm glad you did whatever it is that you did to move on and stop letting the pressure of the wedding get to you. On that note, what are you doing for turkey day?"

"Oh, the usual, except Daphne and I are making appearances at her mother's house and then my parent's house together."

"Very smart, then you won't have to stay long," Heather snickered. "You're already starting to act like a married couple."

"Yeah," Britton giggled. "Hey, I need to get back to my sketches. I have an important deadline this week. If I don't talk to you, I hope you and Greg have a Happy Thanksgiving and tell your parents I said hello as well."

"Sounds good, and you too."

Britton ended the call and shook her head, wishing she could blink her eyes and make the time go by faster. The phone in her hand vibrated and rang once again. This time, Daphne's smiling face was on the screen.

"How did you know I was thinking of you?" Britton asked.

"Call it a wife's intuition," Daphne teased.

Britton laughed. "Maybe Heather's right. We are acting like a married couple."

"What's that supposed to mean? We are one." Daphne paused. "Wait, did you tell her?"

"No. No one knows. It's our secret. She asked me what we were doing Thursday and I told her going to both houses together. She said that's what married couples do, so we're already getting into the swing of things, basically."

"Hmm…I hadn't thought about that. Maybe we should go separately."

"No way. Besides, how is anyone going to know? We took our rings off," Britton replied.

"You don't think you will get nervous or frustrated with your mom and blurt it out?"

"Hell, no. I don't want to be in the room when she finds out we eloped. Nope. I'd rather take my chances and swim with an alligator in a small pond."

Daphne laughed hysterically. "You're a mess," she exclaimed. "But, you're my mess and I love you to death. So, if that alligator eats you, I'll make sure to buy a plot next to yours."

"That's good to know," Britton giggled.

"What are you doing tonight?"

"Well, I had planned to make love to you slowly up against the wall while you called out my name, but…I'll be working. I have to get this damn bar ready to go for the meeting with the owner on Friday. I sort of took an impromptu vacation and messed my schedule all up. What are you doing?"

"Oh, that's just wrong," Daphne huffed.

Britton laughed.

"I'm going to do the final fitting for my dress and hopefully take it home if everything is good," she groaned. "Do you want to trade?"

"Nope."

Daphne giggled. "I miss you," she sighed.

"I miss you too. How about I come over tomorrow night?"

"I think I can wait that long…maybe."

Brides

"Well, I asked you to move in with me. It's stupid to be married and live in two different states."

"Your apartment is too small. I wish the house was ready," Daphne replied.

"I went by there yesterday. It's coming along nicely."

"That's great."

"Did you talk to my father about the transfer?" Britton asked.

"I decided to do it on Thursday."

"Really? Why is that?"

"Well, I'm sure the wedding will come up and that'll be a good time to bring up the notion that we will be moving in together. I was hoping he'd get the hint and suggest it himself."

Britton shook her head. "I'll bring it up. I know he's the company president, but he's also your father-in-law. There's no need to skirt anything with him. He needs to get used to the fact that you're his daughter-in-law and not just an employee anymore."

"Are you sure that's a good idea? You're not exactly involved with the company."

"No, but you're my wife, so it involves me."

"Alright. I guess we'll see what happens."

"You don't sound very sure," Britton stated.

"I'm sorry. I guess I need to get used to being your wife first and an employee here second. Your family is now my family too."

"Exactly, and speaking of family, if I don't get these sketches done, you'll be visiting both of our families alone because I'll be working on Thursday."

"Point taken. I'll see you tomorrow night," Daphne said, hanging up the phone.

Britton turned her cell phone off and walked back over to the drawing desk. She sat down, shaking her head at the clock on the wall. She was definitely in for another late night.

Chapter 23

On Thursday morning, Daphne rushed around getting ready while Britton sat on the couch watching the start of the Macy's Thanksgiving Day Parade.

"Are you going to get dressed?" Daphne asked.

"What for? We're not eating until noon."

"Because I help my mom with the prep and last minute cooking every year. I told her I'd be there by nine thirty."

"Do we really have to go cook? I like to watch the parade."

"What do you do when you go to your parents house?"

Britton shrugged. "I show up with an expensive bottle of wine and watch the parade if it's on. Sometimes my dad and I play chess and watch the football games."

"Uh huh, what about your sister?"

"Bridget always helps mom in the kitchen."

Daphne shook her head and laughed.

"What?" Britton asked, raising an eyebrow.

"What are you going to do when we host Thanksgiving?"

Britton laughed. "That's not happening."

"You don't think your parents will want us or Bridget and Wade to do it? Especially, after we have kids?"

Britton nearly swallowed her own tongue. She gagged and coughed as Daphne rushed over to her.

"Are you alright?" Daphne patted her back.

"Who said we were having kids?" Britton questioned, looking at her with a scrunched up red face.

Daphne smiled and shook her head. "Are you choking to death because I mentioned kids?" she laughed. "Britton, we just got married, I definitely do not want kids anytime soon. Don't worry."

"That's a relief," Britton sighed. Reaching up, she grabbed Daphne's waist and pulled her down into her lap. Before Daphne could protest, Britton kissed her passionately.

"If you start this, we'll never make it to my parents' house," Daphne scolded, pulling back to put a little space between them.

"I'm sure she won't mind if you cancel. You can tell her you're running a fever because you're all hot and bothered by your sexy wife."

Daphne smacked her on the shoulder and laughed. "I love you and I want you right here and right now, but we have plans. So, get your butt up and get dressed before I leave you here," she chided, before kissing her cheek and standing up.

"It's snowing," Britton replied, looking out the window.

"Shit. Are you serious?" Daphne growled. "Now, we're definitely going to be late."

Britton walked up behind her, wrapping her arms around Daphne's waist. "What really has you so flustered, because this person running around like a headless chicken is not the Daphne that I know?"

Daphne leaned her head back on Britton's shoulder. "I guess I'm nervous," she sighed.

Britton walked her over to the window and pulled the curtain further to the side. "Look out there. It's beautiful. It's the first snowfall of the year and I'm happy I get to spend it with you. There's nothing to be nervous about. Okay, so it's the first real holiday we're spending with our families, and we're secretly married, big deal. If our spur-of-the-moment elopement taught us anything, it should be to not let things get us all worked up and to simply live life." Britton squeezed her tighter. "It's our life now. Nothing else matters, but you and I."

"How did you get so philosophical?" Daphne asked, kissing her cheek.

"I don't know. That's usually Heather's job. Maybe she's rubbing off on me." Britton shrugged.

"Hmm…I'd like to ru—"

"If you finish that sentence, we're not leaving this house," Britton interrupted, grinning and raising an eyebrow as if to say 'I dare you'.

Daphne turned in her arms, kissing her softly. "Let's get going before the heat in this room starts melting the snow outside," she murmured against her lips.

~

Thanksgiving lunch and dinner went by as fast as the week had gone. Britton and Daphne had planned to spend the upcoming weekend together, but their families both had other plans. They needed to finish the seating arrangements for the tables, book the limo, book the honeymoon, get the table settings together, and get gifts for the wedding party, which was only Heather and Bridget, but they'd also decided to get gifts for their parents.

Britton worked on the seating arrangements for her family with her mother, then booked the limo and the honeymoon, while Daphne worked on putting together the table settings and took care of buying all of the gifts.

Before either of them knew it, Sunday night had arrived and they hadn't seen each other once. The monotonous last minute details had taken up their entire weekend.

Britton was in the bathroom, filling the tub with hot water and bubbles, with a glass of wine sitting on the sink. She had unrobed and was about to step in when the doorbell rang. Furling her eyebrows together in wonder, she pulled her robe back on and turned off the water, before going to the door. Peering through the peephole, she smiled brightly and pulled the door open.

"Looks pretty cold out there," Britton said, wiping the lightly falling snowflakes from Daphne's pink cheeks.

"I couldn't go all weekend without seeing you, damn it. I hate this," Daphne huffed, removing her jacket. "Where you going to bed?"

"No. I was about to take a hot bubble bath with a glass of wine."

"I knew there was a reason I loved you," Daphne exclaimed, pulling her clothes off.

"Who said you could join me?" Britton teased.

"You did, the day you made me your wife. Now, where's the wine? I've had a weekend from hell," Daphne replied, moving past her in the nude.

Britton simply grinned and watched her walk away.

Brides

Daphne stepped out of the kitchen with a glass of wine. "Well, are you coming?" she asked, walking towards the bathroom.

"Very soon," Britton murmured. "Very soon, indeed," she repeated, following her down the hallway.

Chapter 24

The first week of December went by in a blur. Britton had spent Monday and Tuesday trying to line up the construction crews for the library and get the ground breaking scheduled. Then, Wednesday, Thursday, and Friday she'd worked on the 3-D model of the bar late into the night each night.

She woke up Saturday morning, tired and hungry, still peeling the glue from her fingers where she'd glued them together the night before. She was surprised at how late she'd slept, but thinking back to the hour she went to bed in the early morning, she really hadn't slept much at all.

She got out of bed, started a pot of coffee, and stepped into the shower. The hot spray tickled her senses and relaxed her tense muscles as she washed her hair and soaped her silky smooth skin. Loud pounding on the door was heard when she turned the water off and stepped out of the glass enclosure. She towel-dried her hair and pulled on her robe.

"Don't you have a key?" Britton asked, pulling the door open.

Heather raised an eyebrow at the expanse of cleavage showing in the middle of the loosely tied robe.

Brides

"Do you greet all of your guests this way?" she asked, stepping inside. "No wonder you get so much action."

Britton rolled her eyes and walked away.

"My key is on my key ring by the way. I'm in Greg's car," Heather stated, pouring a cup of coffee.

"Where's yours?" Britton called from down the hall. "Pour me one!" she exclaimed, knowing her best friend all too well. "And why are you here so early?"

"I told you I'd be here at ten and it's ten-thirty," Heather replied, setting Britton's coffee mug on the bathroom counter.

"If the bridal shower is this afternoon and I'm going to that with Daphne, then why are you and I going shopping this morning?"

"You know Bridget and I put together one big bridal shower for you both, but you're having separate bachelorette parties."

"Right...?" Britton looked at her best friend in the mirror as she blow dried her hair. "God, I hate doing this to my hair, but I'll freeze to death if I go out with wet hair."

Heather shrugged. "No one told you to get married in December," she chided.

"Excuse me, I believe you can blame my mother for that one. Anyway, what's with the secrecy?"

"Bridget and I scheduled makeovers for you both this morning. Separate spas, of course. So, surprise, you and I are going to get hot rock massages, tea leaf mud baths, mint facials, manicures, and pedicures!"

Britton scrunched her face. "This definitely sounds like Bridget's idea."

"Of course it was." Heather grinned.

"I'd rather drink a beer and watch paint dry," Britton sighed. "Why the hell didn't you tell me? I wouldn't have taken a shower and washed and dried my damn hair!"

"Oh, come on. It'll be fun. When's the last time you and I did something like this together?"

"Fine, but I'd better be seeing boobs tonight."

Heather laughed hysterically. "You know it's all girls coming to your bachelorette party. Why would I get a female stripper?"

"Seriously?!" Britton growled. "Call Greg. He and Wade owe me for going to their parties. Have them throw something together for later on after this penis party."

"Penis party?" Heather questioned, raising an eyebrow.

"If there's no boobs, then it must be penises. I'm telling you right now, I refuse to drink out of a penis straw or pin one to my shirt. I did that shit for you and Bridget and I'm pulling out my dyke card this time."

"Is that really a thing? A dyke card?" Heather cocked her head to the side.

Britton rolled her eyebrows and ignored her as she walked into the bedroom to get dressed.

"It should be, to keep us from succumbing to the pressure and murdering our straight best friends."

Heather laughed. "I can assure you, you won't have to endure any penises at your party. You're marrying another woman, so I'm pretty sure everyone at the bachelorette party will be aware of the fact that you're a…what do you call it?"

"A lesbian?" Britton asked, dragging out the word lesbian.

"No, the other thing."

"A card carrying dyke?"

Brides

"Yeah," Heather laughed.

Britton stared at her best friend as she pulled her low-heeled boots on and zipped them up.

"Those are cute," Heather exclaimed as she checked out the casual ankle boots with wool lining. "Oh, I bet their warm too."

"Yep. I bought them when I was out at the jeweler having my ring sized. I walked down to Nordstrom while I waited."

"Let's see that ring, since you mentioned it."

"Now? Don't we have to go?" Britton asked, checking her watch.

"Yeah, I guess we should probably go. Our appointment is at eleven," Heather replied.

~

Britton was happy to see Daphne arrive at her apartment so they could go to the bridal shower together. The two hour spa treatment wasn't exactly as relaxing as the brochure said it would be, but it did succeed in taking Britton's mind off everything for a short time.

"Did you get beat with bamboo leaves?" Britton asked, kissing Daphne softly.

"What?" Daphne laughed. "No!"

Britton grimaced. "My spa day was wonderful. How was yours?"

"Actually, we had a lot of fun. Bridget and I have been a few times. I don't particularly care for the mud baths though, so I always opt out of mine and do a spearmint sauna treatment instead."

"You can tell them no?!" Britton exclaimed. "No one bothered to tell me that. I had mud in places I never ever want to have mud again!"

"Aww," Daphne murmured, kissing Britton's pouty lips. "You smell nice."

"It was scented mud," Britton growled.

Daphne laughed hysterically. "Come on, we don't want to be late."

"We could be fashionably late," Britton replied, wiggling her eyebrows.

Daphne shook her head no and walked out the door towards Britton's car.

Chapter 25

The dual bridal shower was at the country club and over the top with extensive decorations, extravagant party favors, and cheesy bridal games. Britton and Daphne received many gifts, most of which were surprises because Daphne had let Britton handle the Nordstrom registry and Britton had let Heather scan everything.

As soon as the party was over, Britton and Daphne loaded the gifts into Britton's car.

"Are you sure everything will fit?" Daphne asked.

"Yes. If it doesn't I'll have Heather take it and I'll get it from her tonight. What are we going to do with a cappuccino machine and a bread maker anyway?"

Daphne shrugged. "That's what you get for letting Heather do the registry," she laughed, wrapping her arms around Britton's neck.

"People are watching," Britton teased, kissing her softly.

"So? You're mine now. I can do whatever I want with you, whenever I want to do it," Daphne stated with a grin.

"Oh, I like that," Britton murmured, leaning back against the side of her and pulling Daphne against her. "What do you want to do right now?" she asked, trailing her lips over Daphne's neck near her ear.

"I want to get out of this cold air," Daphne replied, kissing her once more before pulling away.

Britton pouted. "I'm going to miss you tonight."

"No, you won't. You'll have some bimbo's tits and ass in your face. Just don't touch the skanky ones," Daphne chided.

"Um…have you met your cousin? I seriously doubt she's taking me to a strip club."

"I'm not talking about her. It's her husband I don't trust with you. I remember seeing you the day after his bachelor party."

Britton laughed. "Oh, man you were pissed at me that day. I thought you were going to smack me."

"Yeah, I wanted to beat you to death with that stick that was supposedly up my ass." Daphne shook her head and laughed. "I love you. Have fun tonight."

"I love you too."

"Hey, you two, get a room!" Heather yelled in their direction as she walked down the path towards the parking lot.

"I'd love to, but you and Bridget have ulterior motives," Britton growled in her direction. She held Daphne in her arms, reluctant to let her go.

"After next weekend, you'll be with her for the rest of your life. I think one night won't kill you," Heather teased. "Did everything fit in that race car you call a sedan? God forbid you two ever have kids. You'll have to get a real car."

"Oh, shove it," Britton laughed. "Everything fit just fine, thank you. And would everyone stop saying shit about kids? Can we just enjoy being married?"

Brides

Daphne cleared her throat. "After next weekend, we can enjoy married life all we want and leave the kids to the breeders," she said, nodding towards Heather.

"Don't look at me. I don't want kids any time soon. I married a big one as it is," Heather chided. "Come on, we need to get ready for your party. Bridget started decorating inside for Daphne's party as soon as your mothers both left."

"I didn't see them leave," Daphne replied, looking around at the half empty parking lot. "Or anyone else," she added.

"That's because the two of you were out here dry humping and sucking face like teenagers."

"Gross. No we weren't," Daphne laughed. "Keep her out of trouble tonight and for the love of God, do not let your husband take her to a strip club," she said, backing out of Britton's arms.

"Yes, ma'am," Heather said with a big grin.

Daphne raised an eyebrow. "I don't like that look."

"What look?" Heather shrugged.

'What time do I need to be at your house?" Britton asked Heather.

"I'm headed home now and the party starts in about two hours, so I'd say you have enough time to go home, unload your car, and head my way. Are you staying over tonight?"

"No. I don't plan on drinking a lot."

"I'd better get back inside. Have fun, both of you, and I'm not bailing anyone out of jail tonight." Daphne gave them each a stern look before kissing Britton one last time and walking away.

"Has she met me?" Heather laughed.

"I may have told her some stories from our high school and college days that she missed out on by hating me so much."

Heather giggled and shook her head. "Love/hate is more like it." She wrapped her arms around herself. "Damn, it's cold out today."

"I'll see you soon," Britton replied, sliding into the driver's seat of her car.

~

Britton's bachelorette party was full of laughter, good food, and a couple hours worth of fun. They drank out of covered glasses that were in the shape of boobs and you had to suck the nipple to drink it because that's where the bottom part of the straw attached. They also played silly games like ring toss on dildos that were suctioned to the table, pass the two-headed dildo between your legs from person to person and if you dropped it you were out, as well as a race to see who could get a strap on, literally strapped on, the fastest. Also, everyone got to drawn crude names out of two different bowls to create their lesbian names, then they proceed to add those names to small cards, making everyone in the room a card carrying dyke.

Britton couldn't remember laughing so hard in her life. Heather told her she'd originally planned a stripper, but figured it would be more fun to cut up with old friends and family members and simply have a good time.

Britton was leaving the party when she decided to text Daphne.

Brides

How is ur night going?

Party was good. Home now. U? **Daphne** texted.

Still going. Loads of fun. Boobies galore! Britton replied as she pulled out of Heather's driveway.

Great. LOL Have fun. Daphne wrote back.

Britton set her phone in the cup holder and took the quickest path to the interstate as she cranked the radio.

~

Daphne was about to call it a night when she heard a knock on her door. She turned on the narrow staircase and walked back down to see who it was. She couldn't see through the peephole in the dark, so turned the light on. Britton was leaning against her doorframe with a lazy grin on her face. Daphne smiled and pulled the door open, taking in the sight in front of her.

Britton was wearing jeans, a black leather jacket, a black long-sleeved, button-down blouse with the top few buttons open and the collar pushed wide, showing an expanse of cleavage and the olive complexion of the silky smooth skin of her upper chest. A thin gold chain resting just below her collarbone glistened in the light. Black leather ankle boots completed the outfit. Britton's hair fell in loose waves over her shoulders. She ran her hand through her locks, pushing them back to one side.

"You look like you've been out on the town," Daphne said, smiling.

Britton shook her head no. "I sat at Heather's house, eating food, drinking from boob cups, and playing silly dildo games. No strip clubs; no strippers at all."

"Aww, poor baby," Daphne pouted, pushing the door to let her in.

Britton removed her jacket and rolled her sleeves back a little ways.

"I'm not sure if I believe you haven't been out tonight. You look like you're dressed to kill."

"Call Heather," Britton shrugged. "All I did was change my shirt from earlier today."

Daphne raised an eyebrow. "You really don't know how hot you are, do you?" She shook her head. "If I were your husband instead of your wife, I'd have a semi constantly. Just looking at you drives me wild sometimes."

Britton bit her lower lip and grinned. "You can get dressed and go out on the town with me."

"Why would I do that?" Daphne scrunched her face.

"I don't know. You seem to the think that's my intention." Britton shrugged. "You can show me off and strut around with your chest out because I'm yours and you think I'm so hot that everyone wants me."

Daphne laughed. "Oh, they do want you. You're just too laidback to notice and take advantage of it." She stepped closer, pushing Britton back against the wall next to the door. "Leaving this house…is the absolute…last thing…I want to do," she exaggerated, opening the buttons on Britton's shirt, one at a time. As soon as all of the buttons were opened, she pushed the shirt off

Britton's shoulders' revealing her black satin bra as she kissed her hard.

Britton tried to pull Daphne's shirt over her head, but Daphne grabbed her hands, shaking her head no.

"After making me think you've had strippers in your lap all night, you come here late, unannounced, and dressed sexy as hell," Daphne stated, unbuttoning Britton's jeans. "You're in trouble," she finished, sliding her fingers under Britton's matching panties, teasingly low.

Britton was so wet she could hardly stand up. She went along, submissively allowing Daphne to undress her and fondling her way around Britton's body without letting Britton remove her clothes too.

They made it as far as the bed, before Daphne was inside of her, with Britton begging for release. Daphne teased her, licking her nipples and making lazy circles over her chest with her lips and tongue as her fingers slipped out, circling her wet folds before sliding back in. Britton's hips rocked hard against her, urging her not to stop, but Daphne slowed again, sliding out of her once more, prolonging the cresting wave as long as possible.

Britton jerked her head back, trying to ease her racing heart as she clawed at the sheets under her. She'd never completely given herself to someone so submissively. Her mind was exploding and her body was on fire. This was the most out of control she'd ever been and the feeling was so surreal. She felt like she was going to fly apart into a million shattered pieces.

Britton slammed her eyes closed, unable to watch as Daphne lowered herself, replacing her fingers with her mouth. The feel of Daphne's tongue on her made Britton lose the last of her self-control. Her body trembled and she growled like a caged animal as the orgasm ripped through her body with multiple aftershocks, destroying everything in its path from her head to the tips of her toes.

Daphne rolled to the side, watching Britton pant hard as her body slowly relaxed. She had no idea why she ravished the body of the woman next to her, but seeing Britton at her door had stirred something inside of her, a powerful, possessive feeling that she'd never felt before.

"Who are you? And what have you done with my sweet, innocent wife?" Britton breathed heavily, still trying to catch her breath and bring her heart rate back to normal.

Daphne smiled. "I think marrying you has made me a little different."

"A little? Hell, woman, I thought you were going to kill me!" Britton laughed, shaking her head. "I don't think I'll ever mention playing with strippers again…or maybe I will," Britton grinned, wiggling her eyebrows. "Come here," she said, pulling Daphne into her arms, kissing her softly.

Chapter 26

The last week before the wedding, Britton was busy implementing a few last minute changes the mayor wanted to the library, while also trying to get the permits started for the bar. She was burning the candle at both ends with tight deadlines, but this was the way she loved to work. If it wasn't fast paced and a little bit hair raising at times, it bored her creative mind.

She was nearly late to the rehearsal dinner, sliding into her seat next to Daphne just as the wine was being poured.

"What did I miss?" she asked, kissing Daphne's cheek.

"Nice of you to join us," Bridget muttered.

"Good to see you too, Bridge!" Britton exclaimed loudly with a big smile.

Daphne laughed. "Oh, leave her alone," she chided Britton. "Did you get the permits resubmitted before the courthouse closed?" she asked, sipping her wine.

"I squeezed through the door as the security guard was trying to close it. I damn near had to show him my tits to get in," Britton replied, shaking her head as she reached for her wine glass.

Heather laughed, overhearing her from a few feet away and Bridget shook her head.

"I think everyone's ready for this to be over with," Daphne stated.

"Why is that?"

"Your father barely spoke to me when I arrived. He's usually really nice to me and always makes small talk. What the hell changed?"

"I don't know," Britton shrugged. "My parents are weird sometimes. I think I'm adopted," she whispered with a grin.

Daphne snickered.

~

As soon as the food was served, Daphne's mom began going over the last minute stuff for the next day. Britton's mom interjected a few points and before long, everyone at the table had an opinion about who should walk down first and whether or not they should have both parents or just their father's as originally planned.

By the time dessert had arrived, Daphne's mother had moved on to the subject of the minster, who was the pastor at their church. Britton's family wasn't very religious and Britton and Daphne weren't either, but they'd agreed to have the minister perform the service. What they hadn't agreed to was the actual wording of the ceremony.

"I still think you should allow the Lord's Prayer to be said before the vows," Daphne's mother said.

At that moment, Heather and Bridget sensed a heated discussion coming and they both said goodnight to everyone. Britton's mother walked out with them, to go over a few last minute things. She wanted them to take

Brides

care of the something borrowed, since their rings would be the something blue and something new.

As soon as the three of them were gone, Daphne looked at her mother. "Mom, we decided against it. He should just welcome everyone, say a prayer over us and go on with the vows."

"Do you two even have any vows?" Britton's father interjected.

Britton raised an eyebrow and looked over at her him. "Of course we do. What's wrong? You've been acting weird all night."

"My lawyer called this morning," Britton's father stated. "I told him you'd probably forgotten to sign the prenup since you've been busy all week."

Britton's body stiffened. She'd forgotten alright. "Can he just bring it to the country club tomorrow?"

"No, Britton Marie, he can't," her father snapped. "In fact, he was unable to put it together at all." He turned to Daphne. "Care to explain why?"

"What does this have to do with Daphne?" her mother huffed.

"Should I tell her or should you?" Stephen Prescott asked.

"Tell me what? What the hell is going on?" Daphne's mother demanded.

"She's married to someone else already!" Stephen Prescott exclaimed.

"What? Married to someone? That's absurd. Daphne's never been married," her mother growled. "Maybe you're lawyer—"

"Mom!" Daphne hissed. "It's okay. It's true. I am married."

"I demand that you tell me what is going on this instant. We've shelled out a lot of time and money on this wedding. How dare you not tell us the truth!" Stephen slammed his hand on the table. "Britton, how did you let all of this go on? Did you even know?" he snapped.

"Daddy," Britton sighed. "It's me. She's married to me. We eloped a couple of weeks ago."

"What?!" he yelled.

"Daphne?" her mother questioned.

Daphne nodded.

"This wedding was overwhelming and we went away to find ourselves and remember why we were getting married anyway." She grabbed Daphne's hand. "It was simple, but beautiful. We're sorry we didn't tell anyone. It was very spur of the moment."

"We did it for us," Daphne added.

"Then who is this wedding for?" Stephen growled.

"You. All of you. This wedding is what everyone else wanted and that's why it's still going to happen tomorrow," Britton replied.

"You're damn right it is. Your mother would be heartbroken if she knew what you'd done. She better never hear a word of this," he spat. Shaking his head, he continued. "I cannot believe you didn't sign your prenup, Britton."

"Honestly, I didn't even think about it."

"That's exactly right, you didn't think."

"It's fine. I married her because I love her. You love her like a daughter anyway. This whole family has adored her for years. If anyone should be welcomed into this family without restriction, it's Daphne."

"A lot is at stake here. You have a trust fund and are a stock holder in the family business. If something were

Brides

to ever happen to your sister, Prescott's Grocery goes to you." He shook his head. "You're damn right you didn't think."

"Daddy, do you honestly think I want that? Daphne is your daughter-in-law now and if anything, it should go to her. She's worked for you since she was fifteen years old. She knows the business in and out. Prescott's is her career, not mine. She's the best damn employee you have. Don't you think if I ever get your company, I'll put her in my place? She's my wife and I trust her with everything I have or will ever have. A prenup was never needed. I can't believe you're sitting here putting my own wife down in front of me over money. Keep your damn money and your company. I don't want it." Britton tossed her napkin on the table and shoved her chair back.

"I know you're disappointed, Mom and Dad, but I'm not sorry. I have loved Britton since I was fifteen years old. It felt right the day we said I do on a whim like a couple of kids in love and it feels right doing it all over again tomorrow. It doesn't matter what day we got married on originally or how many times we do it. We love each other and tomorrow, we plan to stand in front of you and everyone else we love and cherish and say our vows again. No one else needs to know our true wedding date. We did that for us and honestly, we never planned to tell any of you because it wasn't for you." She tossed her napkin down and stood up next to Britton.

Together, Britton and Daphne walked towards the door as Britton's mother was coming back in.

"You're leaving?" Sharon asked, hugging them both.

"Yeah. We're tired. It's been a long day and tomorrow will be an even longer one," Britton said, hugging her mother again. "I love you, mom."

"I love you too, darling." Sharon smiled. "I love you both."

Britton and Daphne continued out of the restaurant.

"I know we'd planned to stay away from each other tonight, but we're already married damn it and—"

Daphne kissed Britton's lips, interrupting her. "I love you and all I want to do is spend the rest of tonight wrapped in your arms."

"I'm sorry all of that just happened. My father doesn't look past his name sometimes. He used to call my grandfather Scrooge, yet he acts just like him," Britton stated, as they walked towards their cars.

"It's okay. I understand why he's so upset. They all have a right to be mad. Everyone has been planning this big beautiful wedding and you and I pretty much screwed them over by eloping." Daphne stopped next to her car and turned to face Britton. "I don't regret it. It was the happiest day of my life and tomorrow, I'll have the second happiest day. I'm looking forward to standing up there next to you and doing it all over again."

"I'll never regret it. We could've gotten married in the armpit of hell in front of the devil himself and it wouldn't have mattered to me. You're the only thing in this world that I care about." Britton kissed her softly. "I am looking forward to my teeth not chattering as I say my vows, though." She grinned.

Daphne laughed. "Me too. I nearly froze my ass off on that beach."

Britton giggled. "I'll see you at my apartment."

Chapter 27

The largest conference room of the country club wasn't a church, but it had been turned into a beautifully decorated space with rows and rows of white chairs, separated by a silk runner. White rose petals were scattered down the path and white and blue flowers adorned the end of each row of chairs as well. The guests filed inside, quickly taking their seats.

Heather and Bridget were slightly chaotic with last minute nerves as they helped their best friends finish getting ready. They were also equally shocked at how calm the brides were.

"It's time to start," Sharon Prescott said, poking her head into Britton's dressing room.

"Here we go," Heather nudged her best friend. "Are you sure you're ready to do this?"

"I was ready weeks ago. This is a piece of cake," Britton replied with a smile.

Britton and Daphne's dads walked their mothers down to their chairs. Then, as the music began, Heather and Bridget walked out together and took their places near the makeshift altar in front of the chairs. Then, Britton stepped out of her dressing room, where her father was waiting for her.

"I'm sorry—"

"It's not me you should be saying that to," she replied.

"I know and I just spent the last ten minutes talking to Daphne. I want you to know I'm happy for you, Britton. Whether you got married weeks ago or you get married today, I just want you to be happy. I've never seen you this happy about anything in your life. Your mother adores Daphne and the woman I know in my company is very smart and a great asset, and the woman I've come to know at your side is truly one of a kind. You're very lucky to have each other. I lost my temper last night and I never should have done that, especially not in front of Daphne's family. All I did was cause pain for everyone. I hope you can find it in your heart to forgive me."

Britton hugged him. "Daddy, I don't regret marrying her the way I did, not for one minute. And you causing the mess that you did last night, really hurt me. I've always looked up to you in so many ways." She held her had up when he went to speak. "I know you're disappointed I haven't done things the way you wanted, but this is my life. Daphne and I never meant to hurt anyone. That was not our intention." She peeked out at the mass of people standing, waiting for her. "Can we please forgive and forget so you can walk me down the aisle?"

He smiled and held his arm out. Britton linked hers through his and proceeded next to him as cameras flashed all around. They stopped in front of the altar and he kissed her cheek, before taking his seat next to her mother.

Britton stepped up next to Heather and watched as Daphne and her father walked towards her. A few tears

Brides

escaped her watery eyes at the beautiful sight before her. Daphne was wearing a gorgeous white pearl, sheath style, silk gown with an iridescent embroidered skirt and a sheer tulle back. The dressed flowed out a little at the bottom to add a bit of flare without a train trailing behind it.

As Daphne stepped closer, Britton noticed the pearl and diamond necklace around her neck and recognized it as her mother's.

The ceremony itself went by quickly. The minister said a little speech about marriage, then led a short prayer. After that, he read their vows, instructed them to exchange rings, and finally, pronounced them as a married couple.

Britton pulled Daphne close, kissing her with as much passion as she had the day on the beach when they'd first said I do.

"Is it official now?" Daphne asked, wrapping her arms around Britton's neck and kissing her again.

"Yes, Ms. Prescott, it's official," Britton exclaimed as she grabbed Daphne's hand and walked back up the aisle with her.

~

The reception lasted most of the night as everyone danced, ate the amazing food, and drank freely from the flowing bottles of wine and champagne. Britton and Daphne never left each other's side as they danced here and there and made their way around the room, thanking each of their guests personally.

Just before midnight, they changed into comfortable clothing, leaving everything behind as they headed out to get into the limo that would take them to their hotel suite for the night. Their closest friends and family were gathered in a line, waiting to tell them goodbye.

"I know you leave on your honeymoon in a few hours, but I want you both to know how happy I am. I love you both," Heather slurred.

Britton laughed and hugged her best friend. "Thank you for everything. You're so much more than a best friend to me."

"Congratulations. I'm so happy you're my sister now!" Bridget squealed as she hugged Daphne.

Daphne's parents both hugged her. "We're so very proud of you and happy for you both," her mother said.

Britton's mom wiped tears from her eyes. "My baby girl is all grown up. I couldn't be more proud of you. Daphne, you've always been a daughter to me and now it's official. I love you both," she cried, hugging them.

"Daphne, there's no one else in this world I would ever trust more than you with my daughter's heart. You put the light in her eyes and the smile on her face," Stephen Prescott said. "Britton, I promised myself I wouldn't get emotional, but I wouldn't be any kind of father if I didn't show my baby girl how much I loved her. You two take care of each other and stay true to the vows you took, each and every one of them." He hugged them both. "Oh, and Daphne, pack up your office when you return from your honeymoon."

"What?" Britton replied, slightly stunned.

"You've been transferred to the North Kingstown distribution center." He smiled.

"Thank you!" Daphne exclaimed as they climbed into the back of the Rolls Royce limo.

Brides

Epilogue

Britton and Daphne had just come in from snorkeling in the beautiful turquoise blue water outside of their rented oceanfront villa in the Caribbean, when Daphne's cell phone began chiming with a text message.

Britton was wiping the white sand from her feet when she saw Daphne drop her phone on the chair.

"What's wrong?"

"Bridget knows we eloped. She sent me a nasty message wanting to know why we did it and why I didn't tell her."

"How the hell did she find out?" Britton asked, wrapping her arms around her scantily clad wife. "I really love this bikini on you. Have I mentioned that?" She kissed he lips, then moved to her neck and down her chest.

"What am I going to do? She's pissed."

"She'll get over it. We're going to go make love for the hundredth time. That's what people do on their honeymoon and we didn't get a proper one the first time around," Britton stated, as her phone began ringing on the bar.

"You better answer it," Daphne said, shaking her head.

Britton saw her mother's face on the caller ID. "Hello, mother."

"Britton Marie, I am beside myself right now I'm so mad. Why in the hell did you and Daphne elope? We spent weeks putting that beautiful wedding together!" she yelled.

"It just happened. We didn't plan on it and we didn't think anyone would ever know," Britton tried to explain. "Who told you?"

"It doesn't matter how I found out. I'm so upset with you I can't even think about it."

"Mom, the wedding that everyone wanted, happened. The wedding that Daphne and I wanted, happened. There's no reason to get all upset and angry over nothing. It's over, we're married and that's all that matters."

"We're going to discuss this when you get home," Sharon informed.

"Why don't you go discuss with Bridget about why she was drinking water all night at the wedding," Britton retorted.

"What do you mean?"

"What does it mean when you can't drink alcohol?" Britton sighed. "She was eating a lot too."

"She's pregnant!" Sharon squealed. "Why the hell didn't she tell me? I have to go," she said, hanging up.

Britton smiled and set her phone back down.

"Is Bridget really pregnant?" Daphne asked.

"I don't know and I really don't care." Britton stepped up to her. "Now, we can go enjoy this beautiful scenery and spend the rest of our honeymoon in peace because my mother will be up Bridget's ass." She smiled brightly and leaned in to kiss Daphne's lips as she pulled the string on the back of Daphne's top, causing it to pop open. "Opps," she whispered seductively.

"Oh, your sister is going to hate you," Daphne laughed, tossing the top to the floor.

Britton shrugged. "You used to hate me too."

"No, I never hated. I was in lust with you then fell in love."

"Lust?" Britton raised an eyebrow.

"Yeah, let me show what that is," Daphne said, pushing her down onto the couch on her back. "What the hell is that?" she exclaimed, looking at a package on the table as she sat back up.

"I don't know. It must have been sent to us. Open it," Britton replied.

Daphne tore open the small box, dumping out its contents.

Britton moved to the edge of the couch, noticing a handful of brochures, a thin booklet, and a pink box. She grabbed the top brochure and read the title: *Artificial Insemination.* She tossed it back in the pile and grabbed the booklet titled: *Pregnancy for Lesbians.*

"What is this shit?" Britton exclaimed.

"Apparently, it's a package from your mother," Daphne answered, handing her the enclosed note.

Girls,

I thought this might give you a head start. There's no time like the present to start planning your family.

Love,
Mom

Britton grimaced and took a closer look at the table. An ovulation kit, pregnancy test, and sperm bank brochures were strewn about.

Daphne laughed. "Maybe we should talk about—"

"Noooo!" Britton shrieked.

About the Author

Graysen Morgen is the bestselling author of *Falling Snow*, *Fast Pitch*, *Bridesmaid of Honor*, and *Cypress Lake*, as well as many other titles. She was born and raised in North Florida with winding rivers and waterways at her back door and the white sandy beach a mile away. She has spent most of her lifetime in the sun and on the water. She enjoys reading, writing, fishing, and spending as much time as possible with her partner and their daughter.

You can contact Graysen at graysenmorgen@aol.com and like her fan page on facebook.com/graysenmorgen

Graysen Morgen

Other Titles Available From Triplicity Publishing

Cypress Lake by Graysen Morgen. The small town of Cypress Lake is rocked when one murder after another happens. Dani Ricketts, the Chief Deputy for the Cypress Lake Sheriff's Office, realizes the murders are linked. She's surprised when the girl that broke her heart in high school has not only returned home, but she's also Dani's only suspect. Kristen Malone has come back to Cypress Lake to put the past behind her so that she can move on with her life. Seeing Dani Ricketts again throws her off-guard, nearly derailing her plans to finally rid herself and her family of Cypress Lake.

Crashing Waves by Graysen Morgen. After a tragic accident, Pro Surfer, Rory Eden, spends her days hiding in the surf and snowboard manufacturing company that she built from the ground up, while living her life as a shell of the person that she once was. Rory's world is turned upside when a young surfer pursues her, asking for the one thing she can't do. Adler Troy and Dr. Cason Macauley from Graysen Morgen's best seller, *Falling Snow,* make an appearance in this romantic adventure about life, love, and letting go.

Bridesmaid of Honor by Graysen Morgen. Britton Prescott's best friend is getting married and she's the maid of honor. As if that isn't enough to deal with, Britton's sister announces she's getting married in the same month and her maid of honor is her best friend Daphne, the same woman who has tormented Britton for years. Britton has to suck it up and play nice, instead of scratching her eyes out, because she and Daphne are in both weddings. Everyone is counting on them to behave like adults.

Falling Snow by Graysen Morgen. Dr. Cason Macauley, a high-speed trauma surgeon from Denver meets Adler Troy, a professional snowboarder and sparks fly. The last thing Cason wants is a relationship and Adler doesn't realize what's right in front of her until it's gone, but will it be too late?

Fate vs. Destiny by Graysen Morgen. Logan Greer devotes her life to investigating plane crashes for the National Transportation Safety Board. Brooke McCabe is an investigator with the Federal Aviation Association who literally flies by the seat of her pants. When Logan gets tangled in head games with both women will she choose fate or destiny?

Just Me by Graysen Morgen. Wild child Ian Wiley has to grow up and take the reins of the hundred year old family business when tragedy strikes. Cassidy Harland is a little surprised that she came within an inch of picking up a gorgeous stranger in a bar and is shocked to find out that stranger is the new head of her company.

Graysen Morgen

Love Loss Revenge by Graysen Morgen. Rian Casey is an FBI Agent working the biggest case of her career and madly in love with her girlfriend. Her world is turned upside when tragedy strikes. Heartbroken, she tries to rebuild her life. When she discovers the truth behind what really happened that awful night she decides justice isn't good enough, and vows revenge on everyone involved.

Natural Instinct by Graysen Morgen. Chandler Scott is a Marine Biologist who keeps her private life private. Corey Joslen is intrigued by Chandler from the moment she meets her. Chandler is forced to finally open her life up to Corey. It backfires in Corey's face and sends her running. Will either woman learn to trust her natural instinct?

Secluded Heart by Graysen Morgen. Chase Leery is an overworked cardiac surgeon with a group of best friends that have an opinion and a reason for everything. When she meets a new artist named Remy Sheridan at her best friend's art gallery she is captivated by the reclusive woman. When Chase finds out why Remy is so sheltered will she put her career on the line to help her or is it too difficult to love someone with a secluded heart?

In Love, at War by Graysen Morgen. Charley Hayes is in the Army Air Force and stationed at Ford Island in Pearl Harbor. She is the commanding officer of her own female-only service squadron and doing the one thing she loves most, repairing airplanes. Life is good for Charley, until the day she finds herself falling in love while fighting for her life as her country is thrown haphazardly into World War II. Can she survive being in love and at war?

Fast Pitch by Graysen Morgen. Graham Cahill is a senior in college and the catcher and captain of the softball team. Despite being an all-star pitcher, Bailey Michaels is young and arrogant. Graham and Bailey are forced to get to know each other off the field in order to learn to work together on the field. Will the extra time pay off or will it drive a nail through the team?

Submerged by Graysen Morgen. Assistant District Attorney Layne Carmichael had no idea that the sexy woman she took home from a local bar for a one night stand would turn out to be someone she would be prosecuting months later. Scooter is a Naval Officer on a submarine who changes women like she changes uniforms. When she is accused of a heinous crime she is shocked to see her latest conquest sitting across from her as the prosecuting attorney.

Vow of Solitude by Austen Thorne. Detective Jordan Denali is in a fight for her life against the ghosts from her past and a Serial Killer taunting her with his every move. She lives a life of solitude and plans to keep it that way. When Callie Marceau, a curious Medical Examiner, decides she wants in on the biggest case of her career, as well as, Jordan's life, Jordan is powerless to stop her.

Igniting Temptation by Sydney Canyon. Mackenzie Trotter is the Head of Pediatrics at the local hospital. Her life takes a rather unexpected turn when she meets a flirtatious, beautiful fire fighter. Both women soon discover it doesn't take much to ignite temptation.

One Night by Sydney Canyon. While on a business trip, Caylen Jarrett spends an amazing night with a beautiful stripper. Months later, she is shocked and confused when that same woman re-enters her life. The fact that this stranger could destroy her career doesn't bother her. C.J. is more terrified of the feelings this woman stirs in her. Could she have fallen in love in one night and not even known it?

Fine by Sydney Canyon. Collin Anderson hides behind a façade, pretending everything is fine. Her workaholic wife and best friend are both oblivious as she goes on an emotional journey, battling a potentially hereditary disease that her mother has been diagnosed with. The only person who knows what is really going on, is Collin's doctor. The same doctor, who is an acquaintance that she's always been attracted to, and who has a partner of her own.

Shadow's Eyes by Sydney Canyon. Tyler McCain is the owner of a large ranch that breeds and sells different types of horses. She isn't exactly thrilled when a Hollywood movie producer shows up wanting to film his latest movie on her property. Reegan Delsol is an up and

Brides

coming actress who has everything going for her when she lands the lead role in a new film, but there one small problem that could blow the entire picture.

Light Reading: A Collection of Novellas by Sydney Canyon. Four of Sydney Canyon's novellas together in one book, including the bestsellers *Shadow's Eyes* and *One Night*.

Made in United States
Troutdale, OR
04/27/2025